The body of the M
scythe. Levi had
ered and pink flesh (lamps made the blood on the walls shine like satin. Handprints dragging jeweled trails down drapes and upholstery. Sopping spots on the carpet where lives had drained away.

Levi sat on the edge of the bed. His head in his great scarred hands. He stared out at the wall through his long thick fingers. The rows of fingernails that adorned his forearms twinkled in the dim light. Smoke rose from his mouth and over his head like the cradling arms of a ghost. There was no cigarette in his possession.

There was a tiny gasp as gases escaped from the ragged silver dollar-sized hole in the dead whore's body next to him. It matched the other dozen or so that marked her pink flesh. Two on her ass. One on her belly. Three on her tits. Six on her throat—connected like a necklace. A few on her back.

And the one that got him, her left ear.

He had damn near choked on that earring. He sighed and coughed, and a few straggling plumes of smoke puffed from his lips. He licked them and tasted again the blood that had been drying there. He reached around and patted the dead girl's leg.

"Thank you for the good time, Doll."

He stood and pulled on his stinking jeans and his dusted boots. As he buttoned his shirt, he took note of the ragged scratch, just starting to scab, that ran across his chest.

"I'll be, she got me one."

He smiled and leaned forward and with one quick drag of his fingers, ripped the skin from her left breast. He held it up to his own wounded chest and smiled as it slid home, like it had always been there. Always been his. It looked a lot like a scar.

Like all his others.

Copyright © 2019 by John Boden
ISBN 978-1-950565-56-6
All rights reserved. No part of this book may be used or reproduced in any manner whatsoever without written permission except in the case of brief quotations embodied in critical articles and reviews
For information address Crossroad Press at 141 Brayden Dr., Hertford, NC 27944
A Macabre Ink Production -Macabre Ink is an imprint of Crossroad Press.
www.crossroadpress.com

First Trade Edition

WALK THE DARKNESS DOWN

BY JOHN BODEN

Macabre Ink

THANKS YOUS AND FINE HOWDAYADOS

—I'm certain I will forget people, I always do. It is nothing personal and if you don't see your name but feel you should, please amend the list to include it.

—For Joe Lansdale, for all the influence and inspiration. Thanks is all I got and it don't seem nearly enough.

—For letting me make them characters: Stephen Graham Jones, David James Keaton, Bob Ford, Kelli Owen and Brian Keene, Alycia Hardy, Adrian Shotbolt and Chris Enterline (Sorry about the horse thing.)

—Thanks To:

Linda, Alexander and Sidney Boden, Karen Boden, Ross Boden, Michael Rogers, Donna Kay Boden, Bobbi Jo King, Rhonda Perry, Sherry Cornelius, Dave and Sue Hearn, April Feagley, Sonja Walker, Lori Lane, Alisa Zimmerman, Waylon Glunt, Ken Wood, Mercedes Yardley, Chad Lutzke, Paul Goblirsch and Thunderstorm Books, David Niall Wilson, David Dodd and Crossroad Press, Christopher Seibert, Patrick Lacey, Mike Lombardo, Lex Quinn, John Skipp, Mary SanGiovanni, Eric Beebe, Kristi DeMeester, Michael Wehunt, Somer Canon, Charlene Cocrane, Amber Fallon, Kit Power, Jim McLeod and the GNoH crew, Armand Rosamilia, Christopher Ropes, Mark Allan Gunnells, Bracken MacLeod, James Newman, Louis Lamour, Jack Ketchum (RIP), Zane Grey, Tom Monteleone, Kristopher Triana, Jeremy Wagner, Matthew Bartlett, SJ Bagley,

Christopher Slatsky, Scott Nicolay, Damien Angelica Walters, Dave Thomas, Deena Dib, Rachel Autumn Deering, Jim Lewin and York Emporium, Jason Butler Ferguson, William Grabowski, Skip Novak, Shawn Macomber, Catherine Grant, Wesley Southard, Philip Fracassi, Michelle Garza, Melissa Lason, Adam Cesare, Scott Cole, Jacob Haddon, Jessica McHugh, Ray Mott, Robin Noonan, Stacey Smith, Jim Vajda, Joe Fazzolari, Joe Ripple, Kyle Lybeck, Kevin Foster, Matt Blazi, Olivia Monteleone, Jordan Krall, Steve Wynne, Ceasar Gomez, Frank Errington, Matt Hayward, Stephen King, Kristopher Rufty, Jonathan Janz, Ronald Malfi, Jeff Prettyman, Larissa Glasser, Robert Moore, Wendy Deeley, Lee Thomas, Kate Jonez, John Foster, Dan Padavona, Sam W. Anderson, Matt Weber, Sadie Hartmann, Tod Clark, Andi Rawson, David G. Barnatt, Patti Smeltzer, Tom Sheeder, Joe Ripple and Scares That Care, CV Hunt, Nick Cato, Eddie Coulter...and probably dozens more I'm not thinking of right now.

This is for Pap Pap Corbin

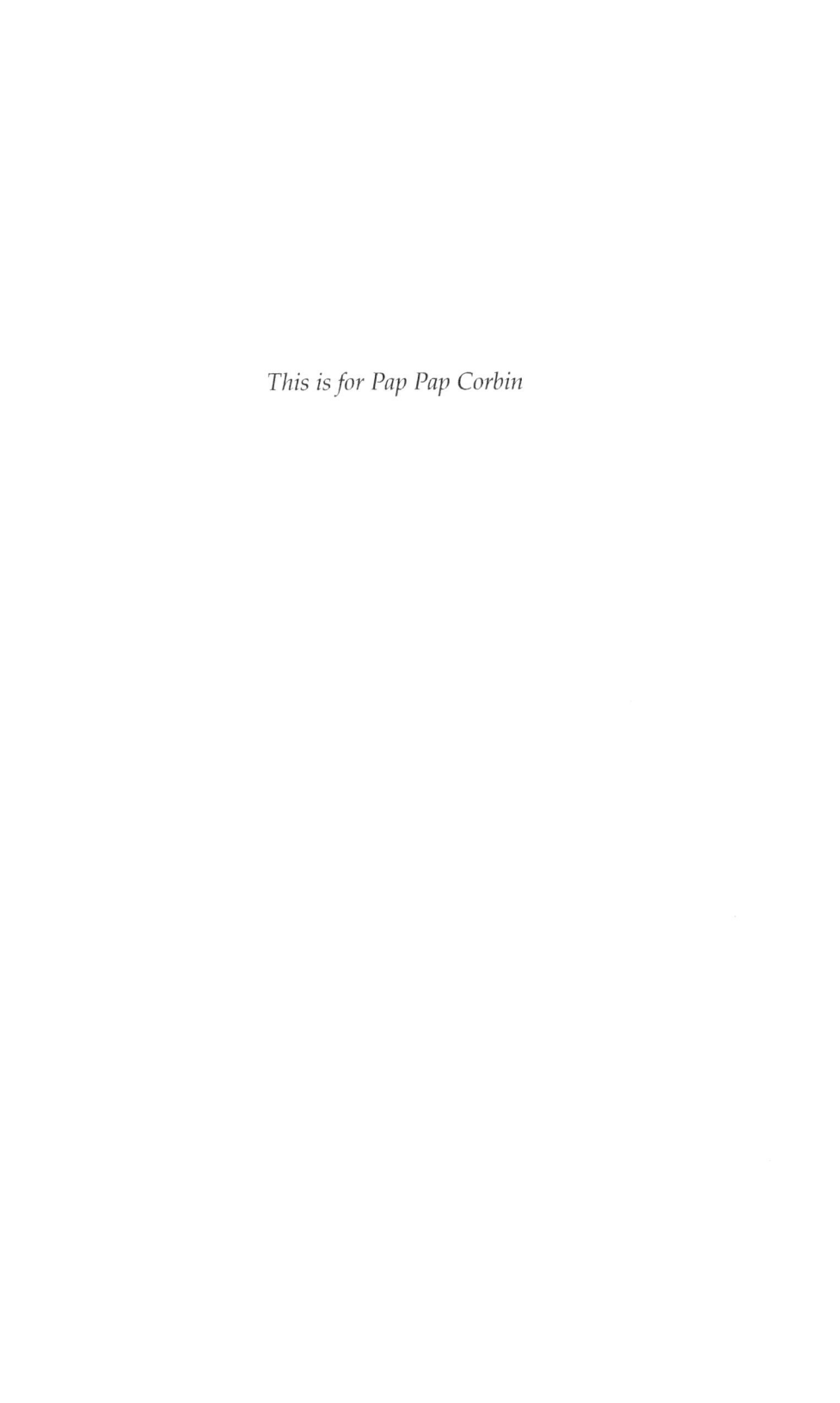

"The trick of functioning with grief is that of remembering and forgetting all at once. Of letting the ghost walk at your side but not block the way."
-Jack Ketchum

"Salvation sat and crossed herself, called the Devil partner"
-Townes Van Zandt

"Men may rise on the stepping stones of their dead selves to higher beings."
-Zane Grey

"For in much wisdom is much vexation, and he who increases knowledge increases sorrow."
-Ecclesiastes 1:18

APRIL 1866

"How old's the farm?" the young child asks—thunder rumbles low outside and the rain sounds like stones on the roof. It sounds like scurrying.

"Older than mine and mine father and perhaps even his and his," the old man replies. The cacophony of the storm trying to smother his voice. The timber walls creak and whine.

"How old is this land?" the child continues. A cloud rolls across the man's face, his features sharpen and draw up like the mouth of a grain sack.

"Older than my memory and older than all of the time I've been here, and I'd wager just as dark."

"Has it always been strange here? Have the shadows always spoke?" The boy's eyes are jewels. Twinkling with a mixture of excitement and fear—terror and awe.

"Yes, sometimes louder and other times barely a whisper. But still the answer is yes. Still always."

The young boy looks at the man and smiles. "It'll be mine one day?"

The man frowns and his eyes appear sad. He coughs a time or two into his fist and then runs his thumb along his bottom lip and it comes away red. "If it'll have you, I reckon. That's the way of the thing. You don't lay claim to it as much as it puts its mark on ye. And low have many been marked." The boy crawls into his bed and pulls the ratty quilt over his head. A few feathers from his pillow flutter in the dim. The old man coughs softly into his hand once more and flings what comes up into the fire. It hisses and sizzles and whispers in tongues.

The smoke goes up the flue and into the night where it is eaten greedily. The boy steals a look to the window and swears he sees pale shapes and fleeting faces. Wide red eyes and mine shaft mouths, stippled with tiny sharp points. He turns his head to the wall and covers it with the blanket. The old man bows his head and outens the lamp with a sour breath. The darkness consumes and its whispers rise and threaten to bury his prayers alive.

MAY 1870

0.

—*T*he boy had been missing his Pa. He always did but on certain days, a certain slant of light or trick of sound would make him think he saw or heard the man. The rusty gate of a voice speaking his name. The rough skin of his hard-worked hand on his head or perched on his shoulder. He missed the man but more so the kindness. After his father died, those things that had been ceased living as well, slowly starving until they resorted to eating themselves. The months since his passing had just been one long sore that wouldn't heal. He heard banging and yelling from inside the house and did his best to ignore it. Levi looked at the point where the sun appeared to be sitting atop the ridge, a fiery king on a great stone throne. He turned away. His dirt-smeared face was wet with tears as he stood behind the small shed. The building that once loomed over him like a boarding house was now merely a foot or three above him. He was growing taller, a sapling in the encroaching dusk. He teetered on the edge and threatened to tumble full long into adulthood at the least provocation. He leaned over the rain barrel that guarded the corner of the tilting structure, the water within seeming bottomless and black as pitch. He listened for his grandfather to bellow for him to hurry up. He needed to clean up for supper as well as remove the signs that he'd been crying. He leaned forward a little and listened. There was no shout, just the smell of the meaty stew wafting from the small window. He took the bar of lye soap from the ledge on the wall and wet his arms. He lathered with the bar, the foam growing gray with the dirt and dried sweat that had coated his limbs. He wiped his frothed hands over his face, closing his eyes tight to guard from the soap. He'd gotten it in there once and would damn sure make certain it never happened again.

Levi scrubbed and then leaned forward, pushing his arms into the cold water. It felt oddly thick and icier than usual. There was the slightly pleasant sting from where the lye had irritated the skin while decimating the dirt. He frowned a little and made to stand back when something touched his hands; a caress, almost, but clammy and rough. He felt them clutched in a grip as cold as the muck at the bottom of a pond and he pulled a little more, panic starting to rise within him. His hands came free easily and he fell backward, spattering himself with frigid water and soapy foam. He looked at his hands and saw red welts. Crescents rimmed in blood, across the tops and palms of both hands. His breath was a vulture caught in a tangle of fence wire. His eyes could grow no wider. From the shadows beneath where the barrel rested on flat stones, from beneath the leaning shed and its sun-bleached sides, a wild glow was growing. Pale and pulsing, it wormed from the dim corners and spaces.

He heard a small laugh and it sounded like it was very wet. He slowly stood and took a few steps back in the direction of the barrel. He looked down into the stilling water, the surface like a slick of oil that glistened like a dark mirror. He stared up at himself, but his reflection smiled. Wide as a valley and with teeth of stone and crumble. Levi opened his own mouth, to allow the gasp a clean escape, but what makes for an escape for one thing, can become an entrance for another—a rope of black water rose from the barrel and was down the boy's throat before he could even move. Levi choked and swallowed the viscous liquid. It was thick, like swallowing the snot from a deep chest cold. The boy gagged and the water broke from the surface and squirmed down his swelling neck. Levi sputtered and coughed as he steadied himself against the corner of the building, the rough splinters gouging his shoulder through the thin plaid shirt. He wiped his forehead and it was quickly slicked with thick sweat before his arm was back at his side. He felt disoriented. His head was swimming in the dark. His soul began to sing, a rising thrum that made him think of the tuning fork that Miss Deering had at school. It was vibrating and making his ribs tremble, his muscles and skin tingle. His teeth seemed to drone and vibrate in their sockets. He heard voices swimming in the pools of his mind and heart, fat and blind from the absence of light. He coughed once more and tasted something like coal dust, like blood and salt, like angry words dying under tongue. He looked to the house. "Boy!"— the bark came like a crack of thunder— "Get thee in here for supper!" The crack of the old man's cane on the window ledge was for punctuation. Levi hung his head and rubbed a sore hand across the scars between his shoulders. His flesh felt warm and tight. Like an egg about to hatch. A twisting knot of words was rolling behind his eyes. Promises and accusations. Threats and litanies. An endless garland of syllables and sacraments both beautiful and profane were tearing him apart and stitching him back together. His eyes burned and he kept them closed to discover his vision wasn't hindered a bit. He slowly made his way to the house, a marionette guided by voices and invisible threads of malice.

—The shadows in the cabin jabbered and dove like Saint Vitus dancers or fainting ladies. Was his grandfather not seeing them? The old man sat and sipped the broth from his bowl, noisily. The candle flicker gave a strobing effect and it did little to calm the boy's churning insides and nerves. He sat on the floor, knees drawn to his chest, head bowed. His ears filled with light words, promises and lies that wore one another's skins. A litany that went on like fences. He barely heard any of the gibberish. It all just tickled his senses like moth wings. The sound of the wooden bowl hitting the floor beside him yanked him to partial focus.

The ancient man before him had just about grown into the wooden rocker that flanked the fireplace. He leaned forward, his nose practically touching the large book that obscured his massive lap. The thick glasses that shielded his eyes and strengthened his vision wavered with flame reflection. "And if ye kill a thing, a creature of blood and breath. If the life from such a thing you take. Your wage is to make it a part of ye. Sew unto thee a swatch of its flesh. For to wear as a badge or a scar." The old man's voice was a trembling thing. His breath, heavy with meat and onion. Palsied hands and brittle bones. He marked the passage with a finger—a long, yellow nail— and closed the book on it. "Now say it back, Levi." The man closed his eyes and leaned in to listen.

"If you kill a thing. Like an animal or a man. Take a life. You must take a piece of it and wear it forever to remind you what you done. Like a badge or a scar." The boy was milk white and rail thin. Scars danced between his shoulders and across his chest. Scars that marked a lifetime of learning. The way he shivered made him appear to be flickering like the candle wicks. The old man's gaze was as sharp as a new knife. He felt it corkscrewing into his guts, loosening his bowels and making his blood boil. He ground his teeth, swallowing the sandy bits of enamel with spit. He was nearly full.

"Close enough." The old man straightened, his spine groaning as did the wood of the chair. He yawned and sat the book on the warm brick of the mantel. The worn-smooth leather shined in the glow. The book bore no name.

The boy stood, suddenly very tall and surprisingly broad of shoulder for his youth, and narrowed his eyes in the dim. They shined like rose-colored glass. "I once read that the Indians say." He paused, a tenuous step on thin ice. "Well, some say that if you kill a man or a beast. You must take a drink of their blood or eat a lump of the flesh, to allow their soul to be free and at rest. Or for them to become a part of you. It was something like that." He never saw the cane swing coming, just felt the hard tip as it connected with the bridge of his nose. The pain was searing and the blood that flowed, thick. Spots like lightning cavorted before him.

"Blasphemer! I'll abide none of that savage talk, Boy." The old man was standing now, as wide as he were tall. A smell of old sweat and spoiled cheese rolled from him. He held the cane out at Levi again. "To kill is a sin. The passage I read ye is about constant reminding and penance. About bearing the cross, About wages, Boy. The yoke of thy sin. An anchor to be dragged for eternity. That blasphemy you speak of is just that. The madness of the devil's tribes." Levi's felt flecks of spittle pepper his burning face. He almost heard them sizzle. He dragged the end of the cane along Levi's shaking arm and it left a snail trail of sticky red. "You understand?"

Levi swallowed and his eyes grew sharp. He lowered his head a bit and stuck out his chin. The blood and blossoming bruise across the center of his face, a diabolical mask. He cleared his throat and spoke— "But the two things are awfully similar, practically the same th—" Whack! Levi spat the broken tooth into his shaking hand. It was so worn from grinding that it looked like a pearl. He put it in his mouth and swallowed it as a pill.

"I once read about people in Africa that ate of their enemies. Some took pieces and wore them to keep other enemies away." Levi's voice sounded slurry from the blood pooling in his mouth. He spat at his grandfather and sneered. He saw that the old man was smiling, too. "I have learned from you. Whatever you read from that book of yours. Learned that it is through pain and hurting we get to all things good." He paused and gulped breaths, "The ladder to heaven has rungs made of razor and wetted with tears." Levi felt consumed with a hotter heat. The heat and unease that had been coiling inside him for hours, days, possibly longer. A fury was building up through his chest and unspringing in fresh muscles that he'd barely gotten to know. Skeins of confusion and uncertainty veined the anger and rage that filled him. He felt a cauldron in his soul and it was roiling. He heard the voices in his ears. They whispered and ordered and pleaded. With a stealth that surprised both of them, he grabbed the end of the cane and yanked it from the old man's grip. He opened his bleeding mouth and allowed the voices escape, they rushed out in a braided whoosh—"I remember the garden. The tree and the fruit. I remember how easy it was to wreck it all. I recall the blackness of the tar and bottom of the sea. I remember the muck between my fins then my fingers and then my toes. I miss the salt and the sandy ashes. I love for the blood to flow as lava…" The old man was trembling. The room smelled of the ammonia-scent of his piss. Levi stood with his jaw unhinged as the voices echoed from his throat. "And I've learned all I need to from you." The color drained from the old man's face as easily as water from a canteen. He held the cane in the light and saw that his blood dotted the shaft. The old man held his hands up before him, like twigs bound with strips of rawhide. Levi smiled and felt the skin at the corners of his mouth split a little. "Now I'm going to teach you a thing or two, we'll see how you take to your lessons." He raised the cane and brought it down. Raised it and brought it down. The old man never got to loose a scream.

—Outside, shadows swirled and danced. In the trees, things flitted and climbed. Skeletal hands of night and blackness wrestled and rolled across the valley. From beneath the shed green lightning flickered. The water in the rain barrel boiled and seethed. The air was filled with laughter and whispers rode the wind. Along the ground and edges of the house, things skittered and crawled in frenzy. There was undulating and slithering and clamoring.

 —Inside, Levi stood in his new suit of glistening red and sheened in perspiration. The cane lay in pieces at his feet. The old man was now a crumpled heap of splintered bone and torn flesh. The room smelled of butchery. Tallow and meat and oh so much blood. Levi leaned down and picked up a tooth that lay near the dead man's wreck of a face. He bent and picked up three more. He bared his own teeth and held the ones from the floor against his bruising gums, feeling the tissue grasp them and cradle them home. He knelt and picked up the rest of them and added them to his own smile. He felt perfect. Unfettered in any way, he felt pure in reason and soul. He was a new day dawning, one destined to end in howling and smoke. He was something strange and new and measured in screams. Levi removed his dungarees and left them in a grue-sodden heap next to his grandfather's corpse. He lay down next to the man who had been raising him. The man who had beaten himself into him, one sermon at a time. The man who was father, mother, savior and sage for the last year or so of his life. Levi nuzzled his head against the slick chest of the cooling man and he whispered himself to sleep. The whispers could hardly be called apologies or prayers. They were bright red promises. Blueprints for a new design. They were the new laws. They were all revealed in his own trembling voice.

SIX YEARS ON

JONES

1.

The swelter of the words, the boil and scald of them, were the only gift he'd ever been given. And he held that gift in the same calloused heart as he did his father's final wheeze, as he did the bullet he took near the end of the war. The bullet that should have snuffed his flame, but instead was slowed by the leather vest and the thick strap of the canteen, and so it did no more than burrow into the muscle of his chest like a tick. Some nights, when feeling a certain way, Jones would sneak a finger or two under his shirt to caress the hard bump that lived there. A way of reminding himself he was lucky to breathe or that he was robbed of death. It went either way sometimes.

He tethered the horse he called Enterline to the dying tree that stooped like an old man's back and slowly walked toward the house. What was left of it. Charred timbers jutted from the mud and ash like the fingers of some great ghoul clawing free of the earth. Jones wished that were the case, he might feel less afraid. He stood and looked at the iron stove, leaning against what was once a wall. How many times had he sat at the table and watched his Ma take pies from that oven? Simmer stews or fry up eggs and bacon upon it. As many days as he had regrets, he'd wager. He closed his eyes and could almost smell the sugary crusts and thick meaty broths. Almost see the blue checked apron she always wore. Her bony fingers grasping the ends of the wooden pin as she rolled dough. Or the flour and dirt under her nails when she'd point to his papers as he would sit and work on his lessons until time to go to bed. After his father had passed, the lessons took ill and quickly died and decomposed into chores and silence. His mother died with his father in a lot of ways. The warmth blew out like a candle. He became an orphan who lived with his paper doll mother in a house full of salty shadows.

 The haggard man was drawn from his memories when the horse snorted, from both ends. He shook his head and walked to where the front door had been. He grasped a handle no longer there and pushed open a door that was fuel for flames days or weeks before. He stepped into the used-to-be kitchen and looked at all the ash. All the mud. Not a single thing remained save for the stove and a few pans. A coffee pot, bent and burnt almost white lay in a drying puddle of muck. The storm had done a hell of a job killing the blaze, assisting the townsfolk with their buckets and pans. Jones breathed deeply and then blew it out through his nose. He knelt and took a fingerful of ashen mud and brought it up and under his nose and sniffed. His mouth turned up, almost smiled then fell back to a down-turned line. He opened it and stuck the finger in, pulling it out clean as he swallowed the sooty glob. He wiped his wet eyes on his sleeve and stood. "Bye Ma," he managed as he stepped over the line of char that was once the wall. He walked quickly to his horse and untied her. She looked at him with sad eyes. He pulled his hair back and adjusted his hat on his head to keep it off his neck, then climbed into the saddle and stole another look at his boyhood home. It was burnt to cinder like so much of him was. He swallowed hard and made a snicking noise through his teeth. With that the horse trotted off and they followed the limping sun.

KEATON

2.

The sky rippled like hides drying on a wire. The wind and distant thunder almost drowning out the constant drone of flies. The drone of the flies almost drowning out the endless tide of prayers and whispers that floated from the church. A hymnal page danced on the meaty breeze like a gull. The hot air simmered and bird shit baked as soon as it spattered the rocks. Shadows cowered in their own shade. It was Sunday, alright.

Keaton rested in the cooling dim of the derelict barn across the road. He looked out at the pasture that flanked the barn, at the dead cattle that littered it. They looked like mountains of black static. Mountains that buzzed and laid eggs that would soon enough be maggots to keep the cycle going. He blinked hard and pulled his gaze the other way. He could see the church through the open door, which was close enough for him. A little too crowded in the house of God these days. He stretched a little and listened to the cracking of his spine. Fingers of sunlight speared the inside of the barn, highlighting dust like ghostly fragments. The barn was far from the sturdiest structure to hole up in, but it was all there was. The wounds in its side had been sloppily bandaged with errant boards and pieces of tin. The hole above his head was patched with a sign for sarsaparilla. The paint was blistered and faded by the sun's eager tongue. Keaton tilted the jar of rain to his lips and sipped loudly. The sulfurous water stung the cut on his lip, but he drank anyway. The stinking water was better than thirsting, for now. He removed his holster so the damned gun barrel would stop poking his thigh. Hell, the bruise that lived there would never fade. He slung it over a shoulder and scooched down against the moldering sacks he was bedding on. The most comfort he'd seen in weeks. He closed his eyes and still smelled the smoke. Heard that Indian woman's screams from behind the wall of flames. Watched the smoke turning and rolling in violent intercourse with the night. He opened his eyes and shook his head, the ache inside seemed to bounce from temple to temple, he sighed.

He stretched once more and closed his burning eyes. Would the smoky sting of them ever fade? Would he ever not see the little house being chewed up by licking orange and devilish heat? The voices from across the road raised in song.

"Onward, upward doth He beckon; Onward, upward would we press…"

Keaton listened until the harmony of the voices dissolved into a low thrum that came to nest behind and between his eyes. He closed them and kept listening, barely aware of the heaviness of the next sigh that escaped his lips and he was asleep before it fell to the ground like a dead mosquito. The sun finished folding itself up, burned itself white and changed its name to Moon and he missed it all.

KEATON & JUBAL

3.

The night went fast, and morning waited anxiously behind it, a precocious child.

"Hey." The small voice was gunshot loud in the quiet barn. Keaton sat up quicker than he should have, his head swam and the ache that anchored there, throbbed. He rubbed the spot on his cheek where his drool had dried.

"Hello yourself," he rasped. His voice was a thing long stowed away. It was like dead spiders dotting an old web in the corner of an unused shed. He coughed into his fist and wiped the red and black swirled phlegm on his hip. He still tasted smoke on his tongue. "Hello, young feller," he said a little louder, steadier. The boy just stood and stared at him. In the curtain of light from the open door, he was a cutout in the shape of a child. A little less bright than the light but still too much so for details to be made out. Keaton went to stand; his numb legs cursed and ignored this decision. He planted his palm against the boards and pulled himself upright. "I mean to apologize for sleepin' in your barn with no askin'. I was raised better than that, I promise you." He swallowed the thick thing living at the back of his throat. Coughed again. "It was gettin' dark and threatenin' to rain again and I was dog tired. I didn't mean to trespass." Keaton replayed the previous evening's events in his mind and recalled there being no house anywhere near the building. Just the vine-covered barn on the one side of the road, the church on the other and a small pasture full of dead cows.

"Ain't my barn," the boy spoke. Clear and succinct. The boy

pulled the door closed and the dimness of the barn ate the light in measured bites. "I don't think Pa will be mad." The boy looked at Keaton, at the gun slung over his shoulder and at the bruises on the thin man's face. Keaton felt his lips warp into a smile, and he waited for the boy to smile back. He did not. "Bet you's hungry, Mister?" The boy asked but it entered the world more like a statement. Keaton stood a little straighter, pain becoming reinforcing rebar that aligned his spine and held him upright.

"I am a bit." The boy turned and made to exit the barn, he waved his arm in a gesture that Keaton understood meant, *Okay then, follow me* and so he did. His stomach growled, sounding like a devil on his tail.

They made their way out through the back of the barn, through a place where a few boards were missing. Keaton had to turn sideways while the boy slid through like a toe through a hole in a sock. The boy took off with great strides through the thick weeds and high grass, his blonde hair bobbing above them being the only thing Keaton could fix on enough to follow. The acre of overgrowth gave rise to a few trees that eventually turned to full blown forest. "Hold Up!" Keaton called as he leaned against a large oak. He was breathing heavy and his lungs burned. He slid a hand inside his shirt, to the makeshift bandages he'd made from a slice of feed sack the night before. It was dry, but he could feel it sticking to the scabbed wound. He knew it would hurt like blazes when he had to pull it free. Maybe they'd find a creek and he could wet it good before, it would still hurt but not as much. He looked at the boy and tried to erase the memories of his wounds and how they came to live with him. The boy just stood in the shade of the trees. The calls and songs of the birds swirling above him. Keaton raised an eyebrow and smiled big and fake. "Gotta name, boy?" He coughed and spat the wad on the leaves that moldered beneath his boots. It shined like a pustular jewel. The boy just stared at him. "You ain't dumb, I spoke at you earlier."

The boy blinked, slowly and then smiled, with half his face. "My name is Jubal. But Boy is okay. Pa always calls me Boy."

Keaton frowned a little, a sad little thing wrapped in wire and struggling. "A name is given for a reason. I'll use yours."

The kid shrugged. He turned and kicked at a pile of rocks that stood beneath a dying willow tree. Before his toes voted different, they were stacked in a small square formation. The one on top shining and black. Obsidian, Keaton remembered it was called. The boy looked back at Keaton, his face a mask of sheepishness and he giggled.

"I kicked the devil in the eye." And upon his saying that, all sound in the forest ceased. The birds, the breeze, even the small rustle of beetle and bug beneath the carpet of twigs and leaves. Absolute silence. It hurt his ears. It was like a hiss behind closed lips.

After minutes that pinched like days, Keaton cleared his throat. It had been a source of raw burning discomfort since the fire. The boy jumped and turned quickly to stare him down.

"That was a mite odd." Keaton croaked as he scratched the bristles of his beard.

The boy smiled that limping smile once more, "You think so?" He dug his toes into the dirt and squinted at the man, "I seen odder. Much odder." He withdrew his toes and began walking off away from their rest spot. A breeze built slowly around them. To Keaton's ears it sounded like voices. Wet whispers from the lips of the dying. He thought he heard his name. They walked and walked and the sour ground devoured their footprints. Unease skipped behind them, scattering seeds.

The woods became sparse, like tufts of stubborn cowlick on a balding man's crown. Rocks jutted at odd angles like teeth and the shrubs and bushes stooped close to the ground. The woods ceased entirely and gave way to a small open field. A small parcel of land with just some high grass and more rocks. A thin trickle of a creek burbled along the one edge. Keaton watched the water shimmer like cat's eyes and felt his mouth fill with spit. He started towards it, licking his lips when the boy halted him. "You can't drink that water."

Keaton stopped and looked at him. "Why is that? I'm thirsty enough to drink the sweat from a fat man's bellybutton."

Jubal grimaced and cocked his little head. "You'd do better to do that." He pointed to the far corner of the field, right where the woods sprung up again like skeletal digits from eroded cemetery soil. Keaton looked back to the brook, in time to see something slink into it. He saw a thick thing. Like a rat's tail but the size of a man's arm. It pulled under the water's surface with a *bloop* and was gone. He saw the boy was headed toward that same far corner and hustled to catch up, peeking back over his shoulder at the creek every few steps. At the strange circular ripples that marred the wide pool of it. He felt it looking back at him. He wasn't very thirsty anymore.

JONES

4.

The horizon was a welt across tanned skin. Raised and red and unforgiving. Further from where the sun sat, nestled like a bloated tick, clouds were visible. Like the last breaths of a dying man on an icy December morning, they floated. There were thickening stalks of smoke rising over the ridge. At least four of them. Like tornadoes suspended in time. Jones could smell that acrid stench of burning wood, a gamier tang mingled in with it, some sort of meat cooking. The smoke pillars rose and congregated with the encroaching storm clouds. Jones sat on the bank, his long legs and feet in the cool water of the pond. He looked down and stared at his feet beneath the slightly murky surface of the water and thought about the morning.

He had gotten the letter while he was working for the railroad. Meaning it was held for him at his boarding house until he made it back into town. His mother was already nearly a month dead by the time he opened the thin paper pouch and read the words. He had made his way into the small town of Lut's Key and taken care of the sale of the homestead property. He wanted nothing to do with it now. It would just be another link in the chain he was dragging. His soul already clanked and rattled. He had to ask the sheriff about the fire. He had been down south fighting and losing. Or perhaps further west seeking his fortune, he said. The salty truth was he was most likely three towns over in a bottle of whiskey or between the legs of a whore. Jones knew shame and he pressed it sharp and clean on his lean frame. His face belied nothing. The Sheriff, a fiercely bearded man named Yates, offered little information— There had been a man named Keaton. A drifter who was helping his mother at the farm. Chores for food and sleeping room in the barn. A man on the run possibly, maybe a criminal or maybe just an innocent tumbleweed. Dependent on who you asked, he had apparently made his way to the old Jones place, forced or asked the woman to hide him and patch him up and then paid her in lead and flame. If he was there at all, he made off before the glow drew the townsfolk with pails and panic. Jones just nodded, he knew no other way to acknowledge. The sheriff gave him one of the posters from the wall. "There's a reward for him. Lotta money. Maybe not a lot but a good bit." The sheriff smiled and then coughed. Once the fit had passed he spit into his handkerchief and stuffed it back into his vest pocket. There was still a little blood on his bottom lip. "Losin' is a helluva bloodhound, son." He patted the worn-looking man on the shoulder and went back into the jailhouse. Jones walked back across the street to where the horse was tied, but in his head, he never took a step.

The tadpoles swirled around his feet and tickled his toes. Jones just stared and listened to the breeze through the brush and the growling in his stomach. He felt the heat of the sun on his back growing weaker and weaker and knew the clouds were devouring the light and the day was withering away. He found it hard to really care. He lay there on the bank and let sleep run her fingers through his unwashed hair.

KEATON & JUBAL

5.

The pair stood in the dank shade of the branches. It smelled of wet earth and pill bugs. Under the canopy of needles and leaves squatted a house, by the most basic of definitions. A square abode. Boards nailed together to form a flat surface, then adjoined to another and another until you had four standing walls and a flat roof atop. Created by the laying of long limbs across the structure, nailed in place. There were easily a dozen hides stretched over, all coated with thick blackish green moss. There was a single window on the front of the dwelling but there was no glass remaining, just thick spider web clotted black with dead flies and wasps. Keaton leaned and tried to peer inside. Shadows holding hands with darkness. Nothing he could focus on and see. He turned to the kid. "This is your house?"

"It's where I live." Jubal snorted and pulled the door open. It groaned, and the swollen timber barely allowed it to swing forward. Keaton gagged as the smell reached out and cuffed him. It was a smell like drying meat and old, damp cloth. River mud and something else. Keaton was no longer hungry. There was buzzing from inside not unlike a droning chorus, like the hymns the night before. He sucked in the biggest breath his bruised chest could hold and entered the shack. The gasp that burst from his cracked lips let that breath escape to flee back out into the daylight, while Keaton just stood there. He could almost hear himself shaking. His eyes watered.

In the corner of the room was a bed. It was covered in linen that was bilge water gray, at least where the sluggish flies weren't congregating. On top of the sheet was a woman. Her skin drawn tight and splitting at points. Her mouth was a ragged cavern, her teeth bright as rhinestones in the darkness. That smile appearing much larger due to the recession of the skin around it. Flies dove in and out of that mouth. His gaze moved down over shoulders that were all point and angle, a nightdress that turned black and wriggling where it became one with the blood-stained sheet. He closed his eyes and listened to the buzzing of the countless flies crawling inside of there. He opened them and looked at the boy. He was sitting on the floor beside a small cradle. Roughly carved from wood. There was a heart painted on the end in dark paint, Keaton hoped it was paint. The boy was humming and rocking it. Keaton summoned all of his will and stepped toward the boy, craning his neck a little to see inside the cradle. Swallowing the bile that was already rising in the terrified anticipation of what would be in it. His brow furrowed.

    The cradle was lined with shreds of white linen. Stained dark in places with what was once bright blood but was now pupil-black spots. Nestled among the scraps were two round things. Matted with thick dark hair. Jubal kept rocking and humming and Keaton knelt closer to the cradle. The smell was terrible. It was different than the reek of decay and rot that filled the room. It was a sour smell like rancid milk and bloated fish. Keaton breathed deeply through his mouth and touched one of the orbs. It rolled over to the side a little showing the seven teeth that lined it, edging a cleft fissure that ran up the side like a deep scar. He saw a divot that almost looked like a closed eye. Something rolled beneath it. "My sisters," the boy answered though Keaton had not spoken a word. "Mama was tellin' me for months, I was gonna have a sister. She could feel it." He smiled and stroked the things in the cradle. He looked up at Keaton with bright eyes and continued. "When it was time, she crawled into bed and sent me to get Pa. She was in terrible pains. He was over at the church, patching the roof. I got him and he come runnin'. We got back and she was dead. Just like that. There were no babies. Pa took and had to cut them out of her and then he put them in the cradle he'd made. Later that night, he went outside and never come back." Keaton could only nod, watching his hand rest on the side of that wretched cradle as the boy rocked it slightly faster.

"Now I'm all they got."

Keaton sighed and looked around at the room. The husk of a woman on the bed, still spawning. The empty shelves and table. The sallow boy rocking a cradle filled with whatever they were.

"C'mon, Jubal, we're gonna get out of here." Keaton stood and shakily held out his hand to the child.

"You still hungry? I have a little cornbread, it's got some mold on it, but it still tastes alright."

Keaton could only shake his head violently, if he opened his mouth again he might vomit. He pulled at the boy's arm and stepped toward the door.

"Wait! I can't leave 'em." The boy was starting to cry. Keaton hung his head and rubbed the back of it with his other hand. He felt the dirt and sweat pill up and roll beneath his trembling fingers. He moved to the bed and pulled one of the pillows from under the dead woman's head. It was relatively unstained. He took a knife from the table and slid it into the pillow and then gently shook most of the feathers and straw from within. Bits floated around amongst the flies like a despicable snow. He then cut a slit in the pillow case and slid it over the boy's head. He gently lifted the two orbs from the cradle and placed them in the makeshift sling. He was surprised that they were warm. And more surprised when the larger one throbbed in his hand.

"Did that thing just lick me!?" his mind shrieked. He wiped his hands on the tablecloth and made for the door. "Now let's go."

He was out in the yard before the boy, looking into the woods behind the house. Wincing when he noticed the ravaged corpse hanging in the tree above the kiln. Birds had nested in its head, bits of grass stuffed the sockets where eyes once gazed from, and the ruins of clothing had grown faded and sodden from the rains, blending in with the colorless branches and leaves. The noose was thick and speckled with bird shit. One of his boots had slid off, taking the putrid flesh of the foot along with it, and it lay on the ground beneath him. Beetles swaddled the shoe and stump like a squirming black blanket.

"Where are we going?" Jubal called as he caught up to Keaton.

"Anywhere that'll have us. Anywhere but here."

"Going back to the church?" Jubal questioned, shifting the sling so that the bulk in it was nestled under his arm.

"Not to the church but in that general direction." Keaton replied and started back across the field toward the place where they first crossed paths.

LEVI

6.

The large man leaned against the fallen tree. He rarely needed much sleep anymore, the constant barrage of voices behind his eyes made it nearly impossible. He'd been listening to them for a few years now, grown accustomed to their tenacity. It was often like trying to think next to a fast rushing river. But every few days, he needed to rest. He sat there and half-closed his eyes. The pink one nestled in the scar just stared. His clothes reeked of smoke and he was clouded in soot. The voices mapped out his prophecy behind a closed lid.

"*Set the lines, the edges of the door. Sink the frame and forge the lock.*" The voices were ancient and clothed in grave dirt and miles of strata. He nodded and groaned a little but did not fully awaken.

"*When the key is in place, we will be home.*"

"Am I the key?" he questioned, his exhausted voice slurred.

"*The key will present itself. You make the door.*"

"I ain't much good at building. My hands aren't made for tools." Levi groggily opened his good eye and saw the world as unfocused as his mind.

"*The tools you will use are those you have mastered. Those we have mentored thee in. Those old ways—pain and suffering and blood and tears. Death is the heaviest of hammers and rage the surest of nails. A stronger door none shall know.*"

Levi hauled his bulk up from the ground. A few beetles fell from his ass into the moist grass and bark and hastily fled. He rubbed his eyes with a ham-sized fist and looked in the direction of the rising sun. He felt the familiar cloak of anger across his neck and shoulders. That easy reservoir that he tapped when violence called for it. He squinted at the sun again. The glare was painful. He wished he could get his hands around that thing and squeeze the shine from it. Oh, to be the man that killed the sun.

JONES

7.

Jones had ridden for nearly twelve hours and was tired. His ass hurt, and his spine and hips ached. He stopped by the tangle of dead trees at the base of the big molar. That's what the rock formation reminded him of, a big back tooth. He tied the horse to one of the lower branches and went about gathering windfall and twigs to build and feed the fire he would need. His stomach growled, and he growled back, it was a game they played. He built the fire and watched it crawl, then toddle and quick as you please start to run. He warmed his hands and poured the beans into the pan. It was the last jar he had. He broke up his last piece of smoked meat and dropped it in. He withdrew the poster from his vest and studied it while his beans bubbled. He burned the man's face into his mind. And without ever taking his eyes from the flames, began to tear the poster to bits.

After reducing the Wanted poster to pieces and eating it with his meat and beans, the man with the long black hair and a very sad gaze bedded down for the night. Jones tried pulling the brim of his hat over his eyes, but it didn't help. Every pop and crackle from the fire was a gunshot by his ear. The smoke that blew over him in the breeze was his mother's ghost prodding and blaming him. He turned on his side, away from the fire, and looked out to where his horse was tied. He watched her eating grass in the darkness. He heard a snarl in the distance, followed by a deeper growl—a yip—and then silence. He closed his eyes and started to count. He made it to forty-three before he was asleep and any dreams he had were nothing to note.

KEATON & JUBAL

8.

Keaton sat against the twisted birch tree's trunk and watched the smoke on the horizon. Looked to be about where the town of Jensen hunkered. The columns were as thick as ancient trees and rose to the clouds like Jack's beanstalk. Keaton almost smiled but then remembered he was talking to the boy. "A little bit of hope is a dangerous thing," he croaked. The smoke escaped his mouth and rolled up and over his face like fog from damper ground.

"You sure you ain't thinkin' of hate?" the boy countered, his left eye winked as he looked at Keaton, the sun behind the man making him a stick of shadow next to the tree.

"Sometimes, there's not much difference." Keaton tried to smile but his lips were cracked and it hurt to do so. The boy stood there, one arm cradling his slingful of sisters while he kicked at the long dead thing that lay at his feet. Whatever it had been, crumbled like a promise.

Keaton dropped his smoke on the ground and crushed it into the dust under his boot heel. He stretched and looked at the boy.

"You ready?" He cocked his head like a dog and the boy nodded. They started out again. The breeze that kicked up felt good on their warm, sweaty skin. Keaton looked to the sky, the clouds were a gauze curtain and behind them was movement, like the palsied hands of a dying man. He breathed deep and felt it rasp his throat. He coughed and spat and never missed a step. Behind him Jubal walked, his sling swaying with the weight of the things it held. From under the cotton shroud a soft cooing purr could almost be heard over the shuffle of dusty feet measuring out dusty ground.

The sun was sliding down the sky, a lapping tongue against a child's face. Keaton heard a tiny whisper and looked over at the boy. He was dozing against the rock. His scrawny arms cradling his sling. Keaton thought he saw a flicker of pink from under the cloth. He stared a little longer but saw nothing to verify it. He lit another cigarette and climbed atop the boulder beside him. The sky grew bruisey and then drained away to full dark. A few tentative stars winked and blinked. Keaton kept staring and smoking.

—*"Restless?!" The man spit when he barked the word. Like the word was snake venom sucked from an enemy's leg or a bit of gristle.*

"I can't be idle. There's more for me than to stay here in Southard." Keaton sighed and shifted his weight to the other foot. He looked hard at the man by the barn door. The man holding the branding iron in his mammoth hand. "You got no claim on me." Keaton barked, his voice was dry grass and dirt blowing against the window. A dust bowl serenade. He looked at the man, daring him to clarify—to speak another goddamned word. They just stared at one another, fish-eyed and crazy.

"Shit, boy. All I ever asked of you was to help around the farm. Your brothers always done it but you always had to be looking for the easy way. Always was an egg sucker." His steely gaze went back to the metal in the fire. It made subtle popping sounds as it began to glow.

"Pa, you know that ain't true." Keaton hooked a thumb under his new gun belt and the gun it held. He thrust his hips out in a subconscious attempt to show off the goods. The older man just leveled a gaze at the boy. His lip climbed up into a sneer.

"You go. You take your fancy outlaw gun and belt and go. I got sons already. Good ones who're willing to help out. You go and find your dreams and easy money and that eventual grave with no marker in the goddamn dirt." The old man spat at him. Keaton wiped the few drops the wind delivered to him from his face and it wet his palm as well as the tears. He held his breath, savoring the horrible words he wanted to

say. He choked them and swallowed their bodies. He clenched his teeth and set his jaw, terrified he would shatter at the sound of an exhale. He metered it out between his teeth, air slowly escaping a knife-kissed lung. He turned and walked to the horse that stood under the apple tree. He called to the old man once more, "Pa." The man paid him no mind. The clang of the hammer on hot iron said enough. Keaton looked at his feet dangling in the stirrups, "I just want you to know…" he paused and watched the man's back as he tinkered with his fire. Keaton closed his mouth and shook his head. He jerked the reins and the horse made off with a slow trot. "…that I love you." He whispered it, even inside his head.—

Keaton looked at Jubal. He was awake now and leaning his head on the rock beside him. "Was you saying something?" The kid asked. Keaton crushed his cigarette into the dirt with filthy fingers and nodded.

"I was thinking about my Pa. About things we said." The kid didn't say a word, just watched him, waiting. Keaton cocked his head and squinted into the growing sunlight at the child. "We had us a quarrel, of sorts…" he paused and decided to tackle it differently. "The tongue is a tricky devil. It can lap and lick and give form to words and promises. It can be dipped in poison or coated in sugar. It can love and it can lie but it can't listen and don't want to learn. It's just a muscle and sometimes muscle is strong and sometimes it just withers away. Sadder still, is when that happens, it don't take its words with it."

The boy just looked at him, a sad and distant look in his eyes. "My Pa said words was traps. You say too many and they'll scatter on the ground around you and trip you up, snarl your legs and lives."

"That is also true," Keaton said as he lit a match and touched it to the fresh cigarette jutting from his lips as though it had sprouted there. He squinted up at the new moon and tried like hell not to recall what had happened to his horse.

LEVI

9.

There was smoke starting to billow, as thick and unforgiving as a brawler's fist, from Hayward's Livery at the end of town. He almost couldn't recall the name of it, he'd been through so many. They were just small bones that connected to form a spine he was eagerly snapping. He was a long shadow flickered in the fire light, making its way to the next building along the empty street. Butler-Ferguson was not a big town. It was barely a small one, just two camps of miners, hoodlums and whores that had sewn themselves together and declared that they were a town. The tall man stood outside the swinging doors of the saloon. *Cocrane's Cups* the branded plank above his head informed. He smiled at the name. It was pretty clever for a shit-town swill station. His face was flat and his eyes widely set, though his skin was tanned to a dark brown by the sun, over his left eye was a swath of pale, a scar of some sort. The eye that nestled there was pink as a piglet. It never blinked or moved, just gazed ahead. The other eye, the bright blue one, darted and danced like a spastic child. The man stood and held a hand over his gun, with the other he held the door and he opened his mouth slightly and drew in a deep breath. The smoke was rich as gravy. He could taste the hay and the wood reduced to smoke and flame. The smell of horsemeat cooking. As soon as he entered, the music and voices stopped. The tall man sidled up to the bar and leaned on it, giving the old wood reason to groan. He scanned the mostly empty room. Less men than he had fingers on both scarred hands—he didn't count the ones in his pockets or in the satchel over his shoulder. He began drumming the thumb of one enormous hand on the mahogany. The balding man behind it scurried over and smiled. "What can I get you?"

"A drink," the tall man spoke, his voice of splinters and dust. "That's always a good start."

"Whiskey do?" the barkeep asked, pouring the liquid into a short glass before he got an answer.

"Just fine," said the stranger and he took the hat from his head and sat it on the bar beside him. The scar on his face began at the hair line and washed down over his left eye like a glacier. It was pinkish pale and looked like wax. The pink eye like a jewel. The barman sat the glass before him and then went back to the other end to resume his conversation with the gentlemen sitting there. The stranger gulped the drink and slammed the glass down hard enough to break it. The sound echoed through the place, over the muted conversations and mumbled gossip. The barkeep spun and looked hard at him.

"Are we going to have a problem?" He questioned as he stepped back towards the stranger and slid a hand under the bar. Like a whip crack, the stranger had jumped half over the bar and nailed the keep's hand to the side of it with his knife. The burnished steel pinning through the bones of the man's wrist. The barman mewled like a soaked cat and his screeches grew until the stranger spit in his face.

"Shut your ass!" The men at the end stood and their hands moved towards their hips. "Just don't…I mean you could, but I wouldn't."

The stranger warned as he leveled his own piece at the barkeeps sweating head. The man stood to his full height and he was a monster. Tall as God and his shoulders were wider than some were tall. The man smiled wide and his teeth shined in the dim of the room. There were far too many of them—all point and a few looked like tarnished silver.

"What's this about?" A small voice came from behind him. The stranger turned and looked and saw it belonged to a shortish man with round glasses. "I want no more trouble, just a reason," the man finished. He was shaking in his boots, literally.

The stranger smiled and scratched his chin with his free hand. "Why do you need that? Ain't bringing him back. Not likely to change a thing that's going to happen today or tomorrow. A reason is nothing but a crutch to break off over someone's skull." He smiled again, impossibly wider. He then pointed and fired three shots, each one decimating the foreheads of the men at the end of the bar. They remained on their stools and the new mouths in their foreheads drooled blood into their beers and on their shirts. The little man screamed but no one moved. The tall man walked over to the table and pulled out a chair. The wood groaned under his weight. "I do this," he said and shot the small man in his right eye. As the little man crumpled to the floor, his broken glasses hanging from one ear, the remaining handful of patrons all started to run for the door, until the man hollered "Stop." Like some schoolyard game, everyone froze in their tracks.

"Just you sit down!" He commanded and damned if they didn't. His smile was as wide and wild as a river. He took the bottle from the middle of the table and poured its contents over those sitting around the big wooden slab. He threw the bottle to the floor and looked at the terrified folks before him. "I tear down. I destroy." He nodded for punctuation as he spoke. He removed something from his vest pocket and sat it on the table before him, then pulled out the little drawer of the box and took out a single match. "Like that old saying, how is it? As you are now, so once was I, as I am now, so you shall be." He paused and furrowed that scarred brow. "That's it." He held the match in his teeth and dumped the rest of the matchsticks onto the table top, scattering them about the whiskey-soaked cloth with his free hand. One of the men made to stand and he pushed the barrel against his head. "Unh-uh." was all he had to say and the man sat back down. The stranger took the match from his mouth and struck it with his thumbnail. There was a sly hiss and a head of flame began to swell. The ugly man smiled. "I apologize for the rudeness, I should have introduced myself. Call me Levi." The match flame touched his thick thumb and hissed out. He popped it into his mouth and chewed then swallowed it. He picked up another.

"That's a real fine name. Real fine," a squirrelly little man with a droopy moustache jabbered. The giant just stared at him, head tilted like a dog when you talk to it.

"A name is just a thing that's given. It's given and taken. Nothing but a handful of letters in the air and off the tongue. Maybe scribbled on paper." Levi countered, and the shaking man's brow furrowed a little. "Let's take a name like Eve, for example. She's the mother of Creation or so the good book tells us. She is motherhood embodied. But then we have the phrase *Eve of Destruction*—this is what we can call a mixed signal." With that, Levi sneered, and the right side of that wicked mouth seemed to touch the corner of his gleaming eye. Teeth stacked like cord wood. "Now, I'm more of a destruction guy myself, so that'd be my favorite Eve." All this chatter was making the already nervous patrons, downright spastic. Levi nodded and licked his lips with a tongue that seemed overlong. In his head, normal young man Levi was screaming, but it was a hoarse mute thing that had been deprived a tongue for a long, long time. He put on the smile again.

"Take the wonderful feeling you have when you build something up. That 'My hands are the hands of God and all this I behold is of my making' pride that you simmer in once you've built something. A coffin. A family. A house. A life. Anything you've made can give you that feeling…" Levi looked at the three men, rooted to their seats by nails of terror. He loomed over them and smiled even wider. "But tearing down is better still. The destroyer is the God no one admits to loving and wanting to be. The clenched fist that breaks the bones or the stomping foot that crushes the kitten. That is the God I aim to please, until I can kick him from his throne and make it my own." He looked at their watering eyes. Their quivering lips. He smelled piss and was certain at least one, more likely all three of them had wet themselves. He struck the match with his thumbnail again. He softened his smile, and damned if his face didn't take on a look of near warmth. "And my dear gentlemen, to that I am well on my way."

He let go and watched the match tumble to the tabletop, where the flame kissed the others and the alcohol and swooned to a blazing dance that engulfed the table and those around it. Levi stepped back and stood at the doorway. The men screamed and flailed and tried to run only to trip over one another and fall to the floor and burn. My, how they burned! The whimpering and sizzling of skin filled the room. Levi turned and stepped out into the newborn night. This was the moment when he always felt most alive.

JONES & FORD

10.

After three days on the go, Jones was about spent. He felt like a fuse that had been lit and then fizzled out before igniting the dynamite. An explosion promised then reneged. He dozed on Enterline (he'd named her after his school yard friend who died in a barn fire when they were kids) and she did her best to keep him headed in the right direction. Above them, the sun was a gunshot wound in dark gray skin, bleeding and rimmed in red spatter. The entire valley was hazed with dissipating smoke that hung like fog. Below them, things wriggled in the earth and spoke in ancient tongues of evolutions and revelations, above them too.

Jones watched the small cabin for about an hour from a safe distance. He saw no one but the old man. He slowly slid from the horse and walked her to the porch. "Old man!" he yelled, trying to sound cordial and not at all intimidating. He was looking for a place to rest and maybe a meal, not a gut shot demise.

He rested a worn boot on the first stone step and hollered once more. "Old man!"

"Ain't no old man here," countered a voice from the side of the building. Jones turned and walked the few feet to the corner of the house and peeked around. There was the geezer, although up close, Jones could see he was not exactly old, more like worn and sickly. His thin long hair fluttered in the small breeze. His eyes smiled before his mouth followed suit.

"I'm sorry, Sir. I meant no offense." Jones apologized, removing his hat to expose greasy long hair. The man sat on a large log, he held a bandana to his lips and began to laugh. It was an appalling sound, starting high and fun but quickly falling to meaty and loose. He began to cough and after several minutes of that he leaned to the side and spat something large and very red into the dust. He wiped his lips and stood, slowly. After a few unsteady steps he placed his hand on Jones' arm.

"I'm Ford, Bob Ford." He wheezed a bit, it sounded like a broken concertina. "I'm not as old as much as I am not very young." He smiled once again and it was a warm creature, soft and purring. Jones felt his mouth doing the same.

"I'm Jones and I'm not feeling very young myself." The two of them stood and smiled a moment.

"You look like a ditch digger's boot. Shit-worn and dirty and not all that proud." Bob offered as he patted Jones on the arm again, gripping him near the elbow and leaning on him to right himself. "You hungry, Son?" he asked as he stepped onto the back porch and further steadied himself against the door.

Jones nodded and then realized the sun was in the man's eyes and he couldn't see him. So he spoke: "Yes, Sir."

"I figured as much, I could use them ribs of yours for a goddamn xylophone." Another thick chuckle from Ford. "And shit, son. My Dad ain't here. So, there's no need for Sir." He laughed a little and kicked at the tom cat trying to get close enough to run into the cabin the moment the door was open. "Git." He hissed, and the cat sped off like a bullet. He went inside, and Jones stood by the porch until the man hollered out the window at him. "I am not serving you out there. Fact, I'm not serving you at all. You want some grub you need to come inside." Jones did just that.

The plate was full. Steam rolled off of the potatoes and the beef smelled divine. There were greens and onions as well, their pungency seemed to clear the scour in his lungs and he breathed deep. Jones felt as though the growling of his stomach could rival that of a bear. He smiled and took a quick bite, it scalded the roof of his mouth and tongue, but he was so hungry he chewed it twice quickly and swallowed it down. He gulped at the glass of water to quell the burn.

"Easy, man. It isn't going anywhere." Ford warned as he

forked a potato into his mouth but not before blowing on it a few times. Jones finished his plate, albeit more slowly, and drank the rest of the water. He scratched at his chin and nodded toward Ford.

"Thank you, Mister Fo…" but was cut off when the man raised a hand and shook his head.

"No, no goddamn Mister. No shuckin' sir. Just Ford. Maybe even Bob at some point. But no Misters, and no more goddamn sirs." Jones nodded and stood. He picked up the plates and took them to the sink which was already filled with three pailfuls of heated water. He shrugged off his coat and let it fall to the floor and once his dirty sleeves were rolled, he started washing the dishes.

"You need not do that, being a guest that I asked in."

It was Jones' turn to cut him off. "I can at least clean the dishes. Maybe myself when I'm done with them, if the water isn't too dirty." Ford sat and watched the thin man washing dishes. The man was tall and lean. Native of blood from his looks. His hair was long and unwashed.

"Fill a pail and I'll get it to heating. You can have a bath when you're done. There's some good lye soap on the sill above the sink. But be careful, it'll take the hide off ya." Bob said, pointing to the empty bucket that sat on the floor by Jones' feet. "There is an actual tub out back, a nice store-bought copper one, I bought it from the catalog a year or so back. It's out by the woodpile. I have some hides thrown over it to keep it from rusting and getting filled with dirt and chicken shit."

"I didn't see any chickens," Jones said, as he rinsed then dried the plate and sat it on the table.

"All birds are chickens," Bob barked. "A lot of people too for that matter." Ford was slowly making his way over to a bed that was along the wall. He eased himself down, springs groaning, and leaned against the mound of pillows so as to maintain eye contact with Jones. He smiled but it seemed tired. He coughed another time or two and then cleared his throat and waited for the younger man to finish his work.

"How is that?" Jones hung the damp towel over the back of the chair and sat down, once again facing his host.

Ford's eyes sparkled, he had been alone a long time it seemed. He began to ramp up his rambling: "I was just getting around to saying that we aren't all that much to be in awe of. Sure, we walk on two legs but we ain't all that far along from drawing pictures on cave walls or poking our shit with sticks to get at the nuts and seeds. We ran on all fours tripping over our dicks and frothing at the mouth like wild dogs. All we've managed to really change is how we walk and the fact that we put clothes on now. But you can see we aren't that far from drooling in our laps and running with the packs. We're insane creations. Made by crazier hands than our own, I reckon. We're dust in the wind, they say, but guess what? We're just as much dust when idle too. A dried out old turd is still a turd. It's just that these turds have thumbs." He paused and took a few deep, rasping breaths. His bandana in hand, poised for its unpleasant business.

Jones had been alone for so long, he enjoyed hearing someone say so much at one time. He nodded so it would continue.

"In the expanse of things, the great big sprawling nitty gritty of the world and all its jive, in that," Ford paused to draw another heaving breath—a thing that teetered and whistled like a breeze from the mines that had burned his lungs black and useless. "In that, my tired friend, we are nothing." He closed his eyes and smiled before continuing. "We're spit in a foaming sea. A lie from the lips of Saints and Sages." Ford wiped the blood from his lips and then wiped his wrist on his shirt front. The dirty cotton drank the red. "We are so small that we tower over our lives like microscopic giants." He laughed at that and winced, his eye turning to slits. "Some carry a big knife because the world's too small," was what he mumbled last. Within a few minutes the wincing expression relaxed and the wheezing turned to labored snoring. Jones rose from the table and went out back to take that long overdue bath.

JONES & FORD

11.

The coughing woke him. It sounded like a storm after a summer of no rain. Dusty and full of grit. He opened one eye and blearily watched Ford hunch over the edge of his bed and spit into the ceramic basin that sat on the floor. It had once been painted white but was now spattered with blood and thick brown sputum. Jones closed his eye and feigned sleep until the man was done coughing. He heard him grab the glass of water from his table and drain it. He swore he could almost hear the hiss as the tepid liquid soothed the scorch of the man's throat. Jones stretched and opened his eyes, making it appear as though he were only then rousing. Ford just looked at him, out over the tops of his glasses and laid the book down on his lap. Jones couldn't see what the title was, even after sitting more upright in the chair he had slouched off to sleep in.

"Look out that window," Ford urged, and Jones did. Then he looked back at the sick man, his brow furrowing. Ford just smiled and sighed. "Yeah, I am well aware that it's filthy. But look out through the dirt at the sun and sky. I like to reckon that's how those above see things down here. 'Cept we're the dirty that hazes their view of a planet of trees and grass and oceans and animals." Ford went quiet and you could almost hear him thinking. "I suspect, what with the railroads and all them new factories in the cities and all, all that smoke from them billowing up in the sky. Before you know it, the whole damned planet will be wrapped in its own dirty window." The smile faded fast and his eyes grew moist. He looked at Jones with an expression of seriousness he had yet to really see. "Thank God, I won't be around to see that. It'd be like looking at the world through my lungs." Jones just sat there, nursing his mug of coffee, not much one can say after a proclamation like that.

After a few minutes that preened like hours, Ford stood up from his bed. His joints popped, and he pushed his wild hair up and over his head. He laid his book on the table and was taking a step towards the kitchen when he heard the scratching at the door. He paused, and Jones felt his hand drift over his gun. Ford was looking his way and shook his head side-to-side and frowned. Another scratch followed by a small whine. Ford smiled and grasped the latch. "Kellianne?" A bark. Quick and shotgun sharp. He pulled the door open and the wolf was inside and on the bed within seconds. She immediately lowered her head and studied the lanky long-haired man at the table. A low growl tumbled from her throat. Jones moved his hand back to his lap and the growling stopped. He swung a hard look at the older man by the door and Ford was still smiling. "That's my wife." He nodded towards the beast on the bed.

"A wolf?" was all Jones could manage.

Ford smiled and went to the shelf by the sink and removed a small tin. He opened it and pulled out a fistful of dried meat.

He took it over and fed the wolf from hand, rubbing her dirty fur with his free one. She raised her head and neck into his touch. Jones was nearly certain he saw tears trickle from her eyes. Ford patted her twice on the hindquarters and sat beside her.

"When I met her, she was a woman. Like you. Indian. Susquehannock. She was lithe and dark and goddamn beautiful." He looked down at her silver muzzle beneath his rough hand. "Still is goddamn beautiful. We met, and she took my heart. Ate it up in bites. While I just stood there smilin' like a damned fool." Ford was far away in his head, rifling through memories. Jones kept listening.

"We spent the night with one another. Holding in the dark and whispering when we was the only ones there. She told me of her family. Of her life and I told her of mine. I was still young and dumb enough to be working the mines. Exchanging breath for dust in secret transactions. She told me, as the sun was rising the second morning, that she'd have to leave. She would return in a month, give or take a day. I asked her why and she wouldn't answer. She dressed and was out the door by the time I got a foot to the floor." Ford looked at the wolf. She now laid on the bed, head on her paws, dozing. He smiled and it was one of the most loving looks Jones had ever seen.

"So I followed. I ended up losing sight of her in the woods and went to the trader's, figured with all the Indians there someone would know her. And they did. I ended up meeting her brother. He told me she was not here. Would not be back for a cycle. I asked what that meant. He explained it to me. He said she was cursed to roam as a wolf until the moon was full. For two days or more, depending on the lunar details. That was the time she could walk among men. Resume existence as her human self." Jones took a slow sip and never broke eye contact with the other man. He had a hard time not smirking. Ford just watched him.

"Oh, I know, it sounds like madness. And it is. I didn't believe it. Not fully. But I searched for weeks and couldn't find her. Then, almost exactly month later, I was in here making supper and I heard a scratch at my door. I opened it and saw a wolf. Just standing and looking at me. I watched as this creature walked into the house and climbed on the bed. I watched as she stretched out and her fur withdrew and left behind flawless brown skin. She positively glistened. I stared as her body turned and swiveled and shifted into the beautiful woman I had met before. I couldn't speak. I just stared. God, she was beautiful." Ford looked at the wolf and his smile was warm. "She is beautiful. He rubbed her shoulder and the wolf closed her eyes. They were wet.

"I asked her if there was a cure. She said she weren't ill. I asked if there was anything that could be done. The answer was always no. It was the way of things. Her price to pay. We spent the next two days knotted like twine and when she was ripe to change back to wolf, I asked her to marry me. She said of course. We had to wait another month for the service which consisted of me and her under the sky making promises. She usually comes home the night before she changes back and we have a day or two of time together before she changes again. She don't always roam. Sometimes she stays here. But more often than not, she has to run. Always running. See, a man can fall in love with another and that other can change-inside or out-and sometimes, that change takes the love with it. Other times, it tempers it into a sharp thing. A strong thing. A thing that can cut all others to ribbons." Bob stroked the gray fur of the wolf's snout. She whined lightly and raised herself into his palm. The man's tears were silent, his smile the most honest thing Jones had ever seen. In his head, he heard words. Almost a prayer, he could not recall from what or where: "*I thank the wolf who taught me how to bite and the sun who taught me how to burn. To bite and to burn, those are hand-holding lovers.*"

He heard himself whisper, "Amen." The wolf whined.

LEVI

12.

The young whore on the bed was dead. So was the one in the next room. And the girl in the room next to that. And in the room next to that one. And the carpetbagger and the old Madam in the lounge downstairs. The body of the Marshal was nailed to the back door with a scythe, Levi had his star-shaped badge pinned to the puckered and pink flesh of his broad chest.

The pale light from the lamps made the blood on the walls shine like satin. Handprints dragging jeweled trails down drapes and upholstery. Sopping spots on the carpet where lives had drained away. Levi sat on the edge of the bed. His head in his great scarred hands. He stared out at the wall through his long thick fingers. The rows of fingernails that adorned his forearms twinkled in the dim light. Smoke rose from his mouth and over his head like the cradling arms of a ghost. There was no cigarette in his possession. There was a tiny gasp as gases escaped from the ragged silver dollar-sized hole in the whore's gut. It matched the other dozen or so that marked her pink flesh. Two on her ass. One on her belly. Three on her tits. Six on her throat—connected like a necklace. A few on her back. And the one that got him, her left ear. He had damn near choked on that earring. He sighed and coughed, and a few straggling plumes of smoke puffed from his lips. He licked them and tasted again the blood that had been drying there. He reached around and patted the dead girl's leg. "Thank you for the good time, Doll." He stood and pulled on his stinking jeans and his dusted boots. As he buttoned his shirt, he took note of the ragged scratch, just starting to scab, that ran across his chest. "I'll be, she got me one." He smiled and leaned forward and with one quick drag of his fingers, ripped the skin from her left breast. He held it up to his own wounded chest and smiled as it slid home, like it had always been there. Always been his. It looked a lot like a scar. Like all of his others.

His boot heels echoed as he descended the wooden steps. He surveyed his work and counted the dead at nine here at the whorehouse. He smiled as he took out the crumpled money from his pocket. He smoothed it and laid it on the desk next to the Madame's head. Her eyes glazed and pale. A fly walked across the left one. He picked up the lamp from the other table and poured the oil around the desk and then threw it across the room. It shattered and slicked the wall. Levi produced a match from his belt. He leaned over and kissed the dead woman's lips, lightly. The fly flew. He thumbed the match head to furious flame and dropped it. And then there was fire. Cleansing and honest and faithful, as the best lovers usually are.

KEATON & JUBAL

13.

They slept near the ruins of a small house devoured by long ago flames and years of weather. House bones of rotting wood and stone stuck up from the overgrown grass and weeds. Keaton hadn't slept a wink all night. This place was strange. The air felt odd and there were noises. Barely audible whispers and voices that vaporized when you stopped to listen. The boy was worn out and slept well, while he sat and smoked cigarettes by the fire. Keaton acted as though he was up mere minutes before the sky started to blush over the mountains. A slight pink-given-to-orange that gossiped that the day was about to begin. Keaton kicked a pebble at Jubal who was sleeping beneath the willow. The kid never moved. Keaton leaned forward—the pull on his bruised shoulder was agonizing—and grabbed another small stone. He tossed it at the sleeping child and it landed on his head with a small thump.

"The Hell?" The boy grumbled as he pulled himself upright and rubbed the spot where the pebble kissed him.

Keaton laughed softly and said. "We can't sleep all day; we have a lot of distance to chew." He stood and began to pull his boots on by the straps. Jubal slowly stood and rubbed sleepers from his eyes. The sun was building steam, spilling light across the field like a seraphim wave.

"Over by that shed, well, what's left of it, is a rain barrel, go wash your face and we'll get going." Keaton held out his hand and the boy hung the sling over it. Keaton grimaced as he looked into the folds and saw the things cradled there. The hair was thick as roots and matted. He stared long enough that he thought he saw them move, slightly. Tiny breaths. The smell was growing weaker but still had that dead fish odor. His stomach lurched, and he turned his head. "Mercy" was all he managed to sputter.

A few yards away, Jubal was standing over the old barrel. It was rimmed with moss and filled to the lip with dark water. The water was so cold that he could see his breath, it was fogging the surface like a window in winter. He leaned forward and had nearly dipped his hand in before he stopped. His reflection was smiling up at him. A very large smile. But Jubal himself wasn't wearing one. He turned and looked to where Keaton stood, holding his sisters. As he turned back, he caught the reflected face doing the same. His skin prickled, and he opened his mouth wide. His reflection did the same, but where Jubal only possessed the normal thirty-two teeth, his reflection had rows and rows that receded back into a cavernous maw. The boy closed his mouth quick and stepped back.

"Hurry up!" Keaton called, he had slung the sisters over a low branch and was making water on the other side of the tree. Jubal nodded and picked up a stick that lay near his feet. He held it against his side and leaned forward. His face stared up at him, much paler and blacker of eye. Jubal moved quick and jabbed the stick into the water, into the reflection's eye. The face opened its mouth and the surface rippled and as Jubal let go of the stick and it sank into the stagnant depths of the barrel, the water began to turn darker, swirls of red emanating from the raw socket his reflection now possessed, Jubal raised a hand to his own eye and felt it was still intact. He stepped back and kicked the barrel with all his strength, tipping it from the flat stones it rested on. The water gushed and soaked into the dry soil. It was red as berries and smelled of copper and sugar. Jubal was back with Keaton and they had started walking by the time the grass began to blacken.

JONES & FORD

14.

"We're nothing of importance, that's what I can tell you. We're fingerprints is what we are. The grave is a bar man's rag wipin' us clean away. Until that time, we're always right there, inches away from the end of the line and never once allowing it to teach us a goddamn thing."

Ford's sermons always seemed to stagger back to mortality and ignorance, Jones learned this quickly. The man would start talking about all manner of things but by the wind-down, it was always we don't matter—we're dying-we are stupid. Jones still smiled and closed his eyes and just listened. He felt that a lot of it had to do with the years of ache and lonely the man had saved up inside. He seemed to be trying damn hard to get it all out in his dwindling time, so he could at the very least die happier. That thought murdered the trace of the smile Jones was still wearing.

On and on went that syrupy voice, edged in decay and steeped in knowledge… "One day, you'll look up at the sky. It will be bruised and pregnant—full of stars like little fish. Wet and gasping and fat with cancer and Christian thought. All the sounds will stop and in that pulsing lilac moment—frozen on your fingertips— you will have to decide where you belong." Jones opened his eyes and he was alone in the room. He looked around and saw the door was slightly open and he heard Ford out in the yard talking. He had dozed off to the cadence of the man's words, a rhythm that wormed beneath his brow and hummed him to sleep. He felt a little bad about the poor manners of it but knew Bob would harbor no ill will. He stood and put on his hat and stepped out into the thin gauze of the day.

Ford stood over near the leaning structure that he called a shed. It sat cocked like a drunkard's hat. The door hung open like the mouth of a skull, and with the crudely made windows that's what it looked like. Bob had a shovel in his hand and he very slowly and meticulously set about digging. The shovel bit into the dusty soil with a skritchy sound.

"What are you doing?" Jones asked, his voice sounding quite loud.

"Making my bed."

"More of your grave talk?" Jones tried to play it off as a joke but felt something catch in his throat.

"Just seems like the time is coming up close. Very close." The man stopped digging and just stared at him. His eyes squinted, and he had that smile on again. "I like you Jones. You're a good man. Owner of a good heart. I can tell these things. I don't want you to have to do it. Hell, you might make it too short and I'll have to spend my death with curled up toes like a goddamned elf." Jones smiled as he turned his back to the digging man and he made his way to the shed. He found another rusted shovel and then he, too, began to dig.

After a few moments, Ford stopped and used his shovel as a crutch, propping up his sweating and sagging self. "While I thought that I was learning how to live, I have been learning how to die."

"Leonardo Da Vinci." Jones responded, and Ford smiled widely and nodded.

"Very good. Thou art learned." This was followed by laughter.

"You know he invented many things. And had plans for many others. Things that have since come to pass and some things I suspect we will see in short time. Mechanical insects and flying machines." Bob held up a shaking hand and waved it to stop Jones from talking.

"I've told you about myself. How I fed my breath to the mines and married a wolf. How I always wanted to be a father but never had the chance. How time is a mother fucker and a goddess to be coveted and hated at the same time." He stopped and drank some of the cool air.

"You've told me about yourself, Jones. You amble and ride on with no clear path. A leaf on the breeze. If you continue to tie your being to the tails of rats and the wings of vultures, you will follow them to a definite dark demise. This path you're on. It won't end well."

"I'm fairly certain of it."

"But you're still gonna go that way. This man you're after, you don't even know if he killed your Ma."

"There is truth in that. Maybe he didn't, maybe I don't really care. Maybe on the great slate one number erased is made up for by another?"

"Killing an innocent man to balance the scales. Brother, that is no way to live. In fact, I'd call that more than a little fucked up."

"I'm nearing the point of willful blindness. I've seen so much for so long. Little of it any good."

"Are you certain you'll kill him?"

"No. I am certain I'll find him. I am fairly certain I will speak to him. And after that, we'll see what happens. Maybe he is innocent, and I will be able to tell. Then we will begin carving a different path."

"You're a strange one, Jones. But meeting you has brought some joy to me. Being married in dog years, I'm lonely often. It's been nice having an ear to bend with my rambling. A person to share space and meals with. A person whom after these last weeks I can call a friend. All of that is worth more than all the gold in China." He chuckled at himself and held up a hand as his laughter turned to another storm of coughing. Jones stood patiently, wincing at the harsh sound. "I want to thank you." Bob managed and Jones saw his wide smile stained with bright red, which was daubed away with a brighter red bandana.

Jones felt his heart crack and his eyes grow moist and all he could manage to say back was "You're welcome."

KEATON & JUBAL

15.

The man with a frame like rusting wire leaned against the tree, uncoiled almost. He drove two fingers into his pocket and retrieved the watch. Its chain was kinked and it was tarnished and did not shine in the feeble sun. He opened it and smiled and then put it back in the dark denim pocket where it lived. "What time is it?" Jubal hollered from the rock he hunkered against.
"This watch doesn't know. Been broken for a long, long time."
"Why'd you look at it then?"
"Well, it was given to me by someone important to me." His grin fell as it tried to sprint. He paused and grabbed the fleeing smile by its tail and put it back on. "The hands are froze at twenty till two, that means it's correct at least twice a day. I just got no way of knowing when that would be." Keaton smiled, and the boy took the sling from over his head and nestled it against the rock, in the large pool of shade it and he threw.
"I don't understand time," the boy spoke.
"I don't think anyone really does." Keaton took a swig from the canteen he had found-and-filled at the abandoned miner shack the night before. "I guess it began with the sun and the moon chasin' one another. The stars and the world a'spinnin'. Someone got to counting things and made a notion that there was time and it was passing. Crawling and eating and making life go." Keaton sniffed and made a slight wince before he stood straighter and walked towards a burst of shrub that marred the

field to their left. He walked a few yards before he waved his arm and Jubal saw black dots swirl around the air before him.

"Come here!" Keaton yowled.

"I think this is a better representation of time for you, son." Keaton pointed to the dead groundhog in the dirt before them. It was teaming with movement and the shades of dried red and black and glistening green were almost beautiful. The smell, however, was not.

"Time is a dead critter?" Jubal ventured.

"No. But it's what time creates. That dead thing is a day. And them flies are hours, hours eat the day. Them maggots wriggling and swarming in there and the ants fighting for their tiny claim...that'd be minutes and seconds. They eat up the hours. Regardless of how many of any of them minutes, seconds and hours there are, at the end of it all—the days that stitch into months and on into years—at the end of it all, is just a pile of bones and some dusty bits of hide."

"There ain't no way to just keep livin'?" the boy asked.

"None that anyone I know of has figured out yet." The man pulled his hat down a little to shield his blistered nose from the bright sun. "In fact, I'm not so sure that oughta be something to want after."

He started walking back to the rock and tree where they had been resting. Jubal stood but lingered a little while, watching, listening to the wet whispering as the minutes and seconds ate the hours.

LEVI

16.

Above her the sky had soured to cold and stony gray, darker clouds spread across like lichen.

Doc Hardy was behind her office taking down the linens. She'd gotten the blood out of them and the scent of lye was still thick, even outdoors. Being a short and buxom thing, she was all but at the end of her reach trying to get the sheets off the line. She sang to herself as she did this. The woman leaned to the wicker basket and placed the slightly stiff fabric in the bottom. The last linen was hanging, awaiting its turn to be taken down and folded and the woman was about to turn back to it when she was swallowed by the shadow. It blotted the feeble and retreating sun like a closed fist.

"May I help you?" she stammered. Her voice was a little bird in a falling nest. She stared into the face of the large man, but so dim was his shadow, she felt as though she were looking up from the bottom of a well. It smelled like that as well. Moist stones and mud.

"Ma'am, I'm thinking maybe you could help me." His voice was mice in a corn crib.

"I can try. But we gotta be quick. It's going to storm."

"I'm looking for the town of Fallon. I've been through so many flyspeck towns that they all look alike. Can you tell me, pretty lady, am I close?"

"Very much. This is Fallon." She took the clothes pins from the line and dropped them in her apron pouch and pulled the laundry from the line.

"That's good. Real good. It seems quiet and small."

"That it is. Aside from me and the Mercantile down street, there isn't much of a town here at all. A few houses and farms. The blind school down the road."

"I see. I just come from Butler. And then I hit Ferguson. Guess they're sorta the same town—connected like Siamese twins or lovers." He paused, "Figured I'd stop here before I moved on to the next town."

"Haddon. That's the next town. Ain't much bigger than here."

"I like a small town. They're easier."

"To what?"

He ignored her and just smiled with teeth. There seemed to be so many.

"You need any help at all here?" He stepped closer and she was certain his shadow kept moving after he'd stopped, it splashed over her like pitch.

"I'm fine. Thank you. You gotta name?" As she looked up into his face, she noticed the scars. The dead eye. Her skin went icy and she felt her spit dry right up.

"Levi. Levi Keene is what I was born with. But that was well before."

"Before what?"

"I changed."

"Changed?"

"'Fore I got the job."

"What job are you talking about?"

"Cleaning up." He replied and it in no way answered her query.

"What?"

"Setting the edges. Building the door."

"Beg pardon?" There was an edge of agitation in her voice.

"It don't matter." He removed his hands from his pockets. Fingers long as branches. He reached for her.

She turned slightly with the last corner of the sheet between fingers that would not stop shaking. She pulled it down and crossed it to the other corner, the one still clipped to the line. She turned and bent to pick up the half-full basket with her free arm when the shadow moved. Quickly. Before she could scream, the man had the sheet twisted around her throat. Her glasses fell to the ground where he stomped them into the dust. The lenses cracked like a baby's fingers. She flailed and raked at his neck with her fingers, red welts and weeping scratches arrived and the man twisted the linen as one would a tourniquet. Her thin neck bulged as he wrung the life out of her. Her screams slowed until they became hacking little bursts of wet noise. The man slung her over his shoulder and walked towards the building she worked and lived in. When the sheet reached the end of its reach the peg popped free and fell to the ground.

    He laid her on the table. It was covered with a not-quite-white sheet that was clean but stained in spots. "You will die on the whispers of others who have died here." He spoke, almost trance-like. His lips never moved at all, the words just crawled from his mouth like ants. "Death is stacked on this table like cordwood." Levi shook his massive head and his hat fell from it. The girl was still alive, he watched her ample breasts rise and fall, slightly with every labored breath. He opened her dress and pulled it from her body. Her skin was as startlingly white as the sheets wanted to be. A small birthmark sat on her shoulder. He pulled out the topmost drawer and found it filled with knives and needles. He closed his eyes and dragged his hands through the contents. The small saw looked like a toy in his enormous paw. Once he took it to her breasts, he found that it cut just like the real thing. She came awake quickly and her screams were ungodly. He kept working until they ceased.

KEATON & JUBAL

17.

"Keep still, dammit." Keaton mouthed at Jubal as they lay flat against the short hill. In the distance the groundhog was working at eating the rotting squash. There had been a farm here at one time, with a garden. The house and barn were long reduced to charred ruins and the garden was strangled with weeds and shrubbery, but the more tenacious vegetation prevailed. There were some squash vines and some tomatoes that, while somewhat stunted, still yielded. Keaton very slowly cocked his gun and drew a small breath. He held it and pulled the trigger. Yards away, the groundhog dropped. Half of its ratty face disappearing. Jubal looked at Keaton as they stood.

"He never saw that coming," the boy spoke with a smile and a half a laugh.

"Ain't nothing funny about that. It's the same for all of us. One day we're just happily eating our pumpkins and then who knows, Pow! You're faceless and dead." Keaton walked with big strides.

"You killed a lot?" the boy asked.

"It's all a lot. Hell, one time is often too many." Keaton sighed, "Never on purpose."

"Really? By accident?"

"I never killed anyone. I have, by way of misfortune of presence been the cause of a demise or two. "

"I ain't sure what that means."

"Means that I've never killed a man myself, but I've gotten people killed."

"Like in the war?"

"It's always like in the war, Son. Always fighting and always sides and no matter which side you're on, it's the wrong one." Keaton had stopped where the dead animal lay. He bent and picked it up. Its head a mess of bright red and white. There was a sizable turd hanging from its ass like a dark brown tongue. He shook the carcass until it broke free and fell to the ground.

"But now we have meat and we can have some of them small tomatoes and the squash the little bastard didn't get." Jubal walked faster to catch up and nodded. His slingful of sisters bounced on his hip. A thin sound like a giggle floated from the linen. Keaton pretended not to hear it. The boy slid his face down into the folds and whispered to the things it held. Keaton heard soft wet noises in response. It made his gorge rise.

"We oughta cook that 'hog with the squash and tomatoes. Maybe find some wild onions or clover," Jubal offered.

"You been a cook?" Keaton half-smirked at the boy.

"I helped my ma all the time. She said groundhog is too gamey to eat on its own. You need to veil it with other flavors." He paused and looked at the man who now stood, holding a near-headless varmint before him. "She said it just like that." He looked off into the air for a moment. His lips turning down slightly before raising into a sad smile. "If we had a kitchen and stove, I could make us up some bread. She taught me that too." Keaton smiled at the boy and laid his free hand on his shoulder.

"Well, then I guess that's how we'll do it. Go find some onion. Gotta be some in the weedy mess." Jubal wandered off to the far part of the was-a-garden. Keaton pulled out his flick knife and went to work separating the dead groundhog from his skin. It was a tedious and unpleasant task.

FORD & JONES

18.

The dying man was sleeping on the bed. His hand lay across his chest like the skeleton of a small animal. His light snoring had given way to a ragged wheezing hours ago. Each breath was an arduous chore that seemed barely productive. Less than six feet away sat Jones. He sat with his arms folded and his head tilted, dozing, but listening to his friend struggling to remain among the living. Ford had hoped to make it another few days, to see his beloved Kellianne when she returned. It was looking less likely with every grating gasp. Jones stood and walked over to the sink where he got and wet the towel that lay there. He took it over and swabbed the man's forehead. In the dusky light of the room, he fancied he could literally see the moisture evaporate from Ford's hot skin. The room was heavily scented with acrid sweat and a sweetness that Jones always associated with death being near. *"Sweet death's breath smells of lilacs"* was a line he had read when he was younger. It seemed close to truth right now. Ford's eyelids fluttered, and the corners of his mouth pulled up as he smiled in slumber, even as he fought to draw breath. Jones smiled a little and thought of the conversations and company this man had given him these few weeks. It was the best he'd felt in a very long time. He laid a hand on the sleeping man's shoulder. The muscle there was trembling. It felt like a daddy long legs walking on his arm. Jones let his hand rest there and he closed his eyes and allowed the muscle to whisper to him through the tiring beats of his friend's heart. Secrets in thickening blood slowly circulating through constricting arteries and veins. The wet whispers that his breaths had become. The clouds that were settling over the blue skies in his eyes. Ford was winding down and winding fast. Jones lightly squeezed his shoulder and Ford groaned in fitful sleep. Jones stood there by his side for what seemed like days, thinking the entire time.

Never one to put much stock in friends or allies, Jones was a loner and a man who barely even liked spending time with himself let alone others, yet this man had wormed his way into the hard muscle that lived in his chest. Jones felt his smile wither like a bad crop. He'd been alone for so very long. Even when he was with family. His father had tolerated him but had little patience for a boy who daydreamed. His mother felt duty-bound to care for him but was there ever really love? Warmth? If there was it had caught ill and atrophied like a lame calf. He recalled it as he was born alone and felt destined to shuffle off the same way. But meeting this man, Ford had been a nicety. A bright spot to see when the burlap was pulled over your eyes. A small treasure found in a sprawling desert. He wiped the sweat away again and stood staring at his new friend. Soon-to-be-late friend. Also, and most importantly, the only friend he'd ever really had. Jones sat back down and laid the damp cloth over his knee. It soaked through the cloth and he didn't much care. He leaned back and closed stinging eyes and almost allowed himself to drift off to the rancid rhythm of the dying man's breathing, but then he heard the scratching at the door.

KEATON & JUBAL

19.

"This isn't too good, is it?" Keaton gnawed the gristle from the small bone and spat it in the fire. The flames jumped and bowed, appreciative for the nourishment. Keaton wiped his mouth on his sleeve. Jubal kept pulling at his portion, his lips slick with melted fat, all the while tearing off little bits of charred flesh from the glistening bones.

"I've et worse." He wiped his mouth on the sling and it left a smear of brownish-yellow grease on the linen. The thing hadn't been white for days now. "Imagine how it'd be if we didn't cook it with them vegetables like I said. Been better had we boiled him first. That gets all the grease out of the meat." The boy fingered the last of his squash into his mouth and swallowed it without chewing. He smiled at Keaton. "Fills the empty though." He belched, and it sounded like it might have tasted bad.

"For a time, I reckon." Keaton said as he stood and dumped the bones and few bits of food left in his hand, into the fire. It sizzled and hissed and then sighed contentedly. "I'll be back. That ain't settling well," and with that the man walked, briskly, to the small and tilting outhouse that stood at the crease of the hill bottom. Jubal watched him enter and tried not to hear the not-so-pretty sounds in the quiet dusk.

The boy looked at the cottage. A hole in its roof like a large mouth. Bats flew from it and darted in the feeble light. The front window was broken, and the door was a swelled tongue. The timber faded to the grayish tan of bible pages. He looked at the little house and his eyes glassed, and he fantasized about them fixing it up and calling it home. He liked Keaton. The man was kinder than his father had been. Maybe kind wasn't the right word, nicer maybe. His father was almost old when Jubal came along and he didn't want to take the time to be what the boy needed. A teacher and preacher, father and friend. Once in a while all of those things but most of the time, none of those things were what he had seen in his father. A man who was a scarecrow. He hung on his pole and scared away the birds of happiness and the crows of contentment. He just hung still and waited for a boy to make a move or speak out of turn and then he'd pounce. By the time his Ma had taken with his sisters, his pa was getting better. He had been trying. He was almost a good pa when he wasn't drinking. But that wasn't nearly often enough. He remembered all the times he sat alone in the dirt behind the barn, playing with ants or drawing in the soil with sticks. His parents' voices fluttering from the windows like heavy doves. He'd give anything to hear them again.

Jubal was swimming through his memories, their warmth thick and pulling like a pond filled with molasses. His arms growing weary and aching. He found he couldn't quite recall what his mother had looked like. He remembered her sugary voice. Her bright little eyes like dollops of blueberry jam on soft bread. But not her face, not her arms that used to embrace him and keep him safe. When he thought on that, he was confronted with that husk of a thing in that horrible nightmare bed. Swaddled in flies and buzzing bloody sheets. The tears came and Jubal let them. He only really came back to the present when the outhouse door opened and Keaton walked across the darkening yard like a man made of cornstalk—long and tall and whispery. Jubal wiped his eyes and pretended to be asleep. In short order, he really was.

KEATON & JUBAL

20.

Even though the end of the day was coming and even though it was starting to cool a bit, from their distance and through the waves of heat rising from the ground, the wagon was still big. It looked like a circus animal. Tall slatted sides and a flat roof turned the long wagon bed into a house on wheels. As they made their way closer, it grew even larger. Keaton held his hand out a little from his side, a gesture Jubal knew meant to hang back and be cautious. So that's what he did. He stopped and crouched in the high grasses and watched the man walk slowly to the side of the wagon. He stepped around from the back and paused at the strange sounds that came from the wagon. He quietly gripped his fingers over the slats and peered into the back of the wagon. The hand that came down on his shoulder caused him to yell and he may even have peed a little in his britches, but he wouldn't ever tell. Keaton spun around and out from under the grip of the giant beside him. His hand went for the gun in the holster that dangled over his thigh.

"No need," was all the giant said in a voice as thick as honey.

Keaton stared at the man. A lot of him. Easily a foot and a half taller, probably more, than he was and as broad as Jubal was tall. The large man had a face that was nearly all beard, wild and white. Small eyes that shined like ore. His bald head was a nest of scars and wrinkles.

"I'm sorry," was all Keaton could manage before his mind brought back what he had seen in the wagon.

The giant shook his head. "My name is Tiny. Call the boy

and come eat with me. Sit and rest a spell." And at that the big man turned and went back to the fire and the kettle that hung over it. Keaton turned and motioned to Jubal to come forward. He then looked back at the wagon. The slats were close together, but he saw fingers poking out here and there and pulling back in, like worms after a hard rain. His stomach began to turn, and he felt a cold sweat burst from his filthy pores. He paused to read the words carved on the side board of the seat "Tombstone Every Mile" and he shook his head and approached the large man.

"I'm Keaton." He said extending his hand to Tiny, hoping the man wouldn't notice it shaking. Tiny took it in his own, a large fish swallowing a smaller one. "This is Jubal." The large man leaned forward, his barrel chest all but knocking the kettle into the flames.

"How do," Tiny said, "You hungry?"

"Sure are. We ate a groundhog a day or so ago. Wasn't too good but it was better than nothing." Jubal offered. The boy never broke from his gaze or smile.

"Good perspective, Jubal. That's all a man needs a lot of the time." Tiny laughed and it was a kind sound but not without threads of sadness.

Keaton nodded in agreement. "Jubal is a smart kid, I'll give him that."

"Not yours though." Tiny said, the kinder tone had dried up and gone hard. Keaton stared at the old man and took note of the steely gaze he was receiving. Keaton opened his mouth to speak but Jubal swooped in like a crow on freshly scattered seed.

"My ma and pa is gone." he answered as he poked the cinders and flames with a stick as he did so. "My ma died having my sisters. And my pa went away." Tiny frowned and he held out a hand to touch the boy's face. This brought Jubal's attention back to him.

"I believe I met your pa," Tiny said in a near whisper. Keaton felt the hairs on his arms rise and dance. He looked away while the large man stirred the stew as it bubbled in the iron pot. Jubal said nothing and so Tiny continued, "I took him on a trip once." He smiled and looked at Keaton, "A place that not everyone gets to see."

The boy looked as though he were about to cry. "Think my Pa hung his self in that tree cause he wanted to go back to that place?"

Keaton felt his mind scream, *that goddamn kid has known all along what his pa had done and yet he stayed there with those things and with his dead ma! My God!*" He felt something slick rise in his throat. He wished it away and it obeyed. Tiny ran a fat finger across the crying boy's cheek and his smile grew warm again. "I think he needed to go back to that place, Jubal. So, I took him there."

At that Jubal smiled wider and nodded. "That's good then," he said. Tiny stole a glance at Keaton and it spoke volumes without a word ever falling from their lips.

Keaton heard a low groaning from the back of the wagon and upon listening closer heard the sounds of sobbing and whispered prayers. Tiny stood and walked over to the seat of the wagon. He grabbed a bundle of linen and unwrapped some tin plates. He patted each of the horses and walked back to the fire. His knees cracked as he sat back down. He ladled stew into a tin and handed it to Jubal. "Thank ye," said the boy before he began shoveling fingerfuls of carrot and meat into his mouth. Tiny just smiled and looked to Keaton, who took the plate from his hand and spooned his own stew onto it.

"You take my pa to Heaven?" Jubal asked as soon as he drank the broth from the plate.

"I took him where he was meant to go," the old man said. He made it sound a helluva lot nicer than the implications it actually held, those being lost on the boy who seemed happy to be full and to think his pa was in the kingdom of the Lord. Keaton heard more moans from the wagon and watched as Tiny tossed a stone against the side. "No more," he hollered, and the sounds ceased. Jubal continued eating as though he never heard a thing. The smile never left his face.

"You ever been told you look like Santy Claus?' the boy asked as he held out his empty plate for another helping.

"A time or two," the big man replied. "Especially come winter." He ladled more stew for the boy.

JONES & FORD

21.

Jones opened the door and knew what would greet him as he pulled it open. Kellianne stood there, her front haunches lowered slightly, and her head hung lower, almost in shame. Jones slowly held out a hand and she smelled it gingerly and then licked his fingers gently.

"C'mon in, Mrs. Ford," he stepped to the side and allowed her passage into the room. She paused and looked at Bob on the bed. His chest rising and falling, but just barely. His long hair was stuck to his damp forehead in clumps. She turned to Jones and softly whined. Her eyes were watering. "I know," was all he could say. He put his hand on her head and rubbed the spot above her eye with his thumb. She whined once more.

"I'll be outside for a bit," he managed to say as he went out on the porch and pulled the door closed. He sat down on the deck and leaned back against the door. Listening to the sounds that trickled beneath it. The wolf's panting grew louder and more laborious. Her whining elevated to a piercing wail, almost a shriek. He heard snapping and wet sounds—the tearing of rained-on denim. Grunting and then it all tapered to low whimpers. He held his face in his hands and pushed his fingers into his eyes. He did not cry but he felt an aching in his being that was like a small crack in a large dam. He sighed and was about to stand when he heard the voice from the other side of the door. A sweetly husky female voice. A trembling timbre. She simply said. "I'm here. I couldn't let you go alone." And then there was the sound of crying and then his dam gave way and he just sat there in the deluge, feeling helpless and small and noting that those things felt like an old comfortable shirt.

LEVI

22.

The Lacey School for the Blind was the largest building in the village of Bantry. In actuality, it was one of the three buildings that made up said village. It had been built to be a hospital but given the fact that the population never grew to really need more than Doc Hardy, who actually resided in the next town over, that never really happened. So the large building that cut into the hillside stood empty until Patrick Lacey, a man of unlimited wealth and heart, saw fit to donate it as a school for blind children. The town had a few of their own but many of the children who boarded and attended there came from other towns, some as far away as Burnt Cabins or York.

Mister Addie Shotbolt was a kind man but a succinct one. He minced no words and did not sugar coat a thing. He stood on the side porch, smoking his pipe and wishing he'd not eaten that second plateful of mutton. The cramps in his gut were nearly crippling. He heard the step creak to his left and saw the large shadow pull itself away from the rest of the darkness.

"Who goes?" he asked, in more of a bark than he had intended. A cloud of tobacco smoke escaping with the words.

"Only I," was all the shadow offered as it stepped up onto the porch next to Shotbolt and rose to its full height. A tower of blackness. The old man said nothing, and as soon as the shadow stepped into the feeble glow of the gas light, he found he literally could not speak. This, this...person was carved from bad dreams. He was a quilt of scary stories and fearsome fables. Stitched in scars and ratty whiskers. Shotbolt clamped his pipe between his teeth and turned to rush back inside but not fast enough to elude Levi's grip on his shoulder. "Not yet, my friend." The voice was a dank thing—moist and threatening to bite and bite deep. Shotbolt turned and looked into that face. That pink eye twitched in its pale folds of shiny skin. The ear on the left side of his head was large and pink while the one on the other side of his head was small and as brown as smoked beef, with a small gold ring in the lobe. His lips were split and the teeth that lived behind them—dear Christ in Heaven—there were so many of them. Levi nodded, and the old man began to wail. "You do good work here?" that voice was slugs under bare feet.

"Yes. I mean, we try." Shotbolt could barely form coherent words. He was choking on the terror he felt. *Were there more ears down the side of this monster's head?! Why did his hands look as though they had scales?!*

"You want to know what I think about your work? I know what God thinks about it." Levi gripped the man's face and pulled it close to his own. It was only this close that Shotbolt realized that the man's hands were covered in fingernails, adhered to his flesh like the scales of a serpent. The groan that fled his lips was momentous. "Blessed shall he be who takes your little ones and dashes them against the rock!" Levi smiled wide enough that Shotbolt could hear the tissue of his cheeks tear further. "A great lover of children was our Lord, yeah?" Levi sneered.

"No," the old man whined. "Be sober-minded; be watchful. Your adversary—the devil—prowls around like a roaring lion, seeking someone to devour." Shotbolt's voice quivered like a new calf in a cold barn.

Levi stepped back and nodded. "You know your good book, old man. Impressive. But worthless all the same. Don't get me wrong. There are fine lessons in that book. Mighty fine lessons that are wasted on creatures too dumb and blind to see them. Willfully ignorant, it's called. You carry that torch, Brother. Try to light that kindling of the soul and see how much of a blaze you get." The tall man paused and snaked a tongue out over all those teeth.

"What do you want?" Shotbolt gasped, his chest felt as though his heart were trying to chew itself free.

The nightmare man smiled. "I'm here on other business. A higher order of it. I'm here to pave the way for new things by tearing down the old." Levi reached into his pocket and removed his knife. With a flick of his wrist, the blade glinted a dark fuchsia in the light.

"I am a man of God. I am a servant and a guardian to these children." Shotbolt was babbling, tears and snot sheening his face. Levi chuckled low in his throat and then he nailed the old man to the wall. The blade sliding right through the left eye socket and punching through the back of his head into the wood of the door. "I am a man of God…" He tried to continue but the nerves fired their dying currents and his final litany slurred to a stop. The old man shook and there was a slapping noise as his bowels let loose. Levi stepped back before any shit got on his boots. He bent and picked up the pipe from the puddle of mess at his feet. He stuck the stem in the dead man's mouth and it barely held against the man's teeth, but it did. Levi straightened the man's collar and walked around and in through the front door of the building. The remains of Shotbolt's final breaths whistled from him and were lost in the growing night breeze. The moon just hung there, unimpressed.

JONES

23.

Jones sat at the table. Bob Ford lay dead in his bed. Kellianne stood by his side and looked down at him with puffy and swollen eyes. "He was a good man."

"Such a good man, one of the best I have known." Jones concurred. He studied her face, her darker skin like his. Her brown eyes. She was indeed beautiful. She adjusted the sleeve of the shirt she wore. "Never a bigger heart have I known. He took me as I was and never questioned a thing. His path was one of love and caring and he did that for me. Walked that with me." Her lips quivered slightly. "And you?"

"Yes, He did." Jones stood and fingered the brim of the hat in his hands. He looked at the serene face of his friend in the bed. Then into the eyes of the woman he had loved. "I stopped for a night's rest and maybe some food. The man welcomed me into his home and allowed me to stay a while longer. He talked and he listened. And he spoke of many things, nature, ours and the world's. He spoke of love and life. Many times about love, and almost always tied it to you." Jones smiled, and it was a warm fire. "He loved you." He held out a hand and she took it, squeezed it once and dropped it.

"I know." She walked over to the table and picked up some bread and began tearing off ragged pieces and laying them on her husband's face. She did the same with the tomatoes and greens that were idle in the basket on the floor. He walked to the door and grabbed the crate of apples and pears and joined her in laying them around and on Ford's body. She looked at him and smiled.

"You know what we're doing?" she asked.

"I believe I do. The food will absorb his sins, the darkness that was in him. Is in everyone. Though I feel that the amount will be small. This allows him to go on pure and free."

"In other cultures, a person is hired to eat the food, and this removes the sin from existence. We will share this duty, you and I."

"I'll do it myself. I've never been one to feel full." Jones laughed, and it was a profane gesture. Hollow.

Kellianne looked at him and nodded. A shiver rolled through her. "The sun is starting to droop. I will be going soon. I won't be back." She felt her chest hitch as her sobs tried their best to escape her. "You were good to my Ford. You were good to me. You're a good man, Jones. You take anything you need from here and be on your way. Be careful out there. Tenacious is the darkness all around this place these days."

"I will and I know. Seems to be the way of things these days, doesn't it?"

"I have passed so much pain and destruction to get here. Nearly every town has been murdered in its sleep. Gutted and burned like a lamb. The winds reek of smoke and boiling blood. The few left living speak of a giant made of scars who is erasing the world bit by bit."

"That sounds a bit of a yarn." Jones wanted to smirk but the unease in his heart hobbled it.

"I have seen the man, from a distance and he is just that. He is anger and misery. He is man and he is not. I don't know what or why just that he is. I suspect he doesn't fully know either. He's been working to this for a time."

"Is his name Keaton?" Jones asked, trying to conjure up the image of the sketched face of the poster he'd eaten and shat out weeks before.

"This one goes by Keene. Levi Keene." She stopped and winced as another shudder embraced her. "He has burnt entire towns to the ground. He starts at one end and just makes his way through, one building at a time. Killing and burning until he reaches the other end, then he just keeps walking until he gets to the next town."

"That's insane. Why has none of the law—" He started before she cut him off.

"He's killed them all too. He just kills and burns and does it again and again." Jones just stared at her.

"Just be mindful. Be careful. Darkness is a fickle friend, sometimes you must run ahead. Men are always chasing daylight but then there are times when you must walk the darkness down."

She looked out the window, at the hole in the yard. The shovels rusting on the ground. "Don't put him in that hole. He deserves better. Leave him to his bed and set the house alight. His ashes will dance on the winds…and if I am lucky, on my tongue should I lick the air." She broke then and cried for what seemed like an eternity. Jones just looked on feeling very strong yet very small.

Later, once the sun was gone and the moon had staggered in to replace it. Kellianne was gone. Jones had gone outside while she changed and had once again heard the sounds of metamorphosis. After she scratched the door, he entered and she allowed him to pet her, nuzzling her head against his leg. Her eyes were wet and the fur of her muzzle sopping. He knelt and kissed her nose very softly.

"I thank you, Kellianne. For making Bob Ford the man he was. For showing him the thing called love and for always returning to keep it tended." She licked his haggard face and yipped softly. She pawed over to the bed and looked at her husband. His face still handsome but sunken from where he was eaten from the inside out. She stared for minutes and then she ate the bread that was over his mouth. She chewed it slowly and swallowed. She looked at Jones and barked once before bounding out the door. Jones smiled and watched her disappear into the night. He then grabbed the chair from the table side and moved it to the edge of the bed. He sat down and began to eat.

KEATON & JUBAL

24.

Jubal slept in the palsied glow of the fire. His snores were small creatures in the dim. Keaton smoked and nodded as Tiny spoke: "Tell me what happened, David."

Keaton had already opened his mouth to respond before he realized that he'd never told this man his first name. In fact, he didn't recollect giving his or Jubal's names before he'd addressed the boy earlier. His own name he'd never told anyone outside of his kin. He stopped and then kept going. "I lit out when I wasn't much more than a kid myself. I had full britches and an empty head and that is not the best of combinations as you may well know." Tiny chuckled and nodded. "I was on my own for a few years. Mighta only been two years but they gotta way of stretching like taffy, don't they? I worked the railroad for a bit but then they started lettin' us all go and taking on the Chinese cause they could work those suckers for next to nothing. Actually, nothing a lot of the time." The half-smile on his face wilted and he looked at the large man in the firelight with sad eyes. "That's no way to be. I left angry, fiery at the fact that they gave my work to them bastards. Then I saw the truth of it and it hurt my heart. I got paid and was treated fairly, for the most part. They were not. I was then angry and ashamed." Keaton spat into the flames.

"After," Tiny prodded. His eyes twinkled as jewels in the orange.

"I lost my horse. Shit, I still can't tell you where he went or what happened to him. I think I was thrown. There's a lot of gray area in my head until I met the old woman who had a farm outside of Lut's Key." He paused and took a swig of coffee. Tiny nodded. "I stumbled into town, shoulder fucked, and my face and side bruised. I approached the sheriff first, which is always the safest bet. You know how these small towns can be to strangers. Ain't always smiles and back slaps to be sure."

"Indeed, I do," Tiny said and drank from his own cup of coffee.

"And so, he sent me to the doctor who slinged my arm and patched my hurts, and then suggested I head out to the old Jones farm. It was a ways outside of town. Said the lady out there was old and alone and would no doubt appreciate a hand around the place. So that's what I did." Another gulp.

"She was not what you'd call a friendly crone. She was short and sharp of tongue and had no tolerance for idle chit chat. I helped her mend the barn door and I helped her bring in the crops. I was there near to a month before…" Keaton trailed off and stared as though something in those dancing flames had reached out and hooked his eyes.

"I'd decided I was going to walk into town for a drink. I'd been working hard and she fed me well and let me bed in the barn but wasn't much for talking and I was kind of lonely, I guess. So, I went in to the saloon. It was fine. A beer or three and some whiskey. Then I made to be headed back, I knew she'd be hollering at me to get up and to work as soon as that sun so much as stuck a finger over that ridge. I got to the lip of the valley and I saw the glow. I smelled the smoke. I started running and being half drunk musta made that quite a sight to behold." He chuckled once, and it was a foreign thing in the night air.

"I got to the house and it was burning, fierce as a sermon. I hollered for Mrs. Jones, Melissa was her name. But nothing came back. I ran to the barn and when I flung open the door I saw that the horses were dead. Their throats torn open and shining like ice. I didn't linger on it but grabbed a pail and made for the pump. The roof had already caved, and I knew that the woman was dead. I cried a little, maybe. Didn't know her that well but she was kind to me and ain't no one deserves to go like that. I started filling and throwing buckets at that fire and it just kept burning like a bully thumbing his nose at me. That fire was thirsty." Keaton stopped again and looked at the large man across from him. There was a sad line, somewhere between smile and frown and his eyes were damp. The giant nodded.

"I was at the pump for at least the twelfth bucket of water when I saw the shadow strut from the barn. Just what it did, it strutted like a goddamn rooster. I hollered. 'Hey, come help me get this out!' and the man, I could see that it was a man. A big feller. But he just walked away and up into the hillside brush. He was singing or humming, I couldn't quite tell over the noise of the fire eating that house. I just went back to my labor. After a bit, I saw the glow of lanterns and heard horses, so I knew the town was coming to my aid. I ran to the barn to get more buckets and I saw them horses. This time I really saw them. Throats as open as a fish's mouth. I saw my bedding all soaked in the blood. I saw a knife laying on my pillow, crusted with blood. And then I knew. I knew that man I'd seen had done it. He'd killed them horses and he'd set the house alight. And I was as sure as I have ten toes on my feet, that he'd no doubt killed that poor woman too. I felt bad for the fact that I'd hoped he'd killed her before setting the house a fire." Keaton stalled a minute or three.

"I realized the town would think it were me. And really, I couldn't blame them. A wounded stranger who can't recall shit. His bedding bloody and a knife in his possession and a barnful of dead horses and a dead woman and her burning house. I dropped the pail and grabbed the few things I had in there, my belt and gun and I tore outta there. Right out the back of the barn and into the hills that had devoured the stranger minutes before."

"Feel better, talking of it, finally?" Tiny asked, his voice was kind and felt like milk.

"I can't really say that 'better' is the best choice of a word for that question."

Tiny's smile faded, "I suspect not." The big man poured the last of the coffee into Keaton's tin cup. "You know they have posters of you around?"

"I figured as much." Keaton sipped at the brew and grimaced at its bitterness.

"There is also word that the woman's son is looking for you." Tiny sipped his own coffee. "But I think he will soon figure that you're innocent of that particular deed." Tiny poured the rest of his drink onto the ground beside him and laid down on his side. He bent one large arm under his head and looked at Keaton. "Get some sleep. I'll doze a little while but then I've got to move. I deliver on a tight schedule." Almost as punctuation, a murmur of groans escaped from the wagon. Tiny hissed quick and sharp through his teeth and it quieted down immediately. "I'll be gone when you two get up. Be careful and take care of that boy."

Keaton nodded, "I thank you for your kindness and I will."

"And take care of them sisters." Tiny said as he closed those tired eyes. Keaton's opened a little wider.

LEVI

25.

The tall man stood under the canopy of the forest and watched the large building burn. The flames were high, and he almost swore he could see where they singed the moon. He closed his eyes and listened as the screams of the children inside dwindled and eventually were drowned out by the hungry roar of the flames. He flared his nostrils and inhaled deep the acrid smoke of the burning wood and the salty tang of cooking meat. His stomach growled, and he laughed at that. Strings of saliva dangled from his chin. He wiped them on a filthy sleeve and waited a few more minutes to see if any heroes were forthcoming, before remembering that he'd already killed the town. Levi decided to just stand in the glow of the burning school. His back against the shadows or the woods and bask in the glory of his work. His stomach growled once more.

JONES

26.

Jones sat on his horse and watched the small house burn, the small house with his dead friend in its belly. He couldn't bear the thought of putting the man in the earth. There only to be eaten by worms and made one with the silt and stone. He deserved a quicker journey. Deserved to join with the sun and skies he admired. To soar with his ideas and owls. To be part of the night and the stars and blow on the moon. He deserved immortality, but Jones couldn't give him that. He did the best he could. He had read to Ford from one of his books, the words were stiff and sharp like chicken bones, but he chewed them anyway:

"The stitches that muted him were tight—regretful and baleful knots—his words struggled behind bound lips and eventually went mad—eating themselves in the frenzy."

He had read further and as he finished a page he gently tore it from the binding. He stuffed them beneath Ford's rigid body. He whispered promises and pledges as he lit them with a stove match and stood until the linen caught. Watched with wet eyes as the paper curled and fumed and the small flames kissed the sleep shirt then smoldered and took full fire. He nodded and watched a few more minutes until the heat and the stench grew too much and then he went outside. He stood just off the porch and listened to the whoosh as the walls caught and the flames devoured anything that didn't need chewing. He stepped backwards until he was to the small barn where the horse waited. The smoke rolled thick and sour over the yard.

Now, sitting on Enterline across the field, he watched the small house smoke and burn. Jones looked at the sky, more accurately the horizon and the herd of dark clouds that were rolling in, to lose their identity in the black billows from the fire. He smiled at them and glanced back at the ruins of the house.

"Goodbye, Bob Ford," his voice was tar paper and dust.

And with a snicking sound the horse began to trot off, with a very sad and tired man on his back.

KEATON & JUBAL

27.

The boy sat against the apple tree, head in his arms and snoring. The seven cores at his feet, teaming with ants and being dive-bombed by yellow jackets. Keaton lit another smoke and squinted out across the cornfield. The weeds waved in the breeze and out beyond the rows the woman just stood. She was most likely a scarecrow, he surmised. But then in the draft he swore he saw her hair as it danced in the air and her dress as it billowed. She was too far away to make any detail out. Keaton held his hand over his eyes and it helped little. He stubbed the cigarette on his boot heel and stood. His knees cracked like walnuts and he glanced back at Jubal. He was sound asleep. The man started walking across the field toward the lady.

The stalks whispered as he strode through them. His boots losing purchase on the ears that were torn free and eaten by deer and other animals. He heard things scurry alongside him, rows over. He thought he heard voices. He tried not to think about it, but he slid his hand closer to his gun just in case. He paused to catch his breath, the distance much greater than he'd thought. He turned and saw the tree and Jubal beneath it. It seemed to be at least a mile back. He turned and started walking again. He stopped when he was slapped by the stink and heard the squelch of his boot in something wet. He looked down and though his mouth opened for a gasp, no sound would come.

Carcasses. Easily hundreds. Squirrels. Raccoons and possums. Birds and snakes and frogs. Deer and rats and bobcats. He even saw a bear and a few coyotes. They were laid out in a large circle, some places in layers. Their pelts were scabbed with dried blood and their congealing offal made a thick muck of the dirt. The corn around them was taller and leaned over them, almost as guardian. Keaton gagged and spit. He rubbed his eyes which burned from the stink. He looked again at the dead animals. They were all ripped open. Hollowed of their guts, the eyes were gone. Empty sockets that drooled thick gory ropes. Keaton covered his mouth and pressed on, in less than five yards the field opened up into a clearing. Keaton stopped and stood statue still. The air seemed to do the same. Nothing moved nor made a sound. Keaton's ragged breathing sounded like a train in the quiet. The clearing was ringed with more dead beasts. A garland of snakes and field mice. Rats tied tail to tail. So much dark black blood-mud and all of it alive with white wriggling maggots and huge black flies. The sound returned suddenly as a wall of buzzing.

JONES

28.

It felt like he'd been wandering for years. Dog years, seven for everyone and all of them bad. He sat atop Enterline and scanned the view. It never seemed to change. Trees and tangled brush. Weedy fields of high grass and bramble. Occasionally cut with a creek or on even rarer occasion and a river or lake. The skyline always gray and lined with coaly lines of smoke from whatever might be burning this day. The fresh air always snagged with the tang of his sweat and the reek of fire. He dug into his haversack and pulled out a pear. After a few bites he held it down for his horse and she ate what remained in a single bite, core and all. Jones readjusted his hat and dug at a sliver of fruit skin stuck in his teeth. He stared out at the field before him. He settled his gaze on the copse of apple trees near the end of the large derelict cornfield. He almost thought he could make out a person under the one closest. Looked just like a dot from where he was. Jones sat straighter and tugged the strap a little. Enterline started down the slight hill into the valley, toward the apple trees.

KEATON

29.

It was no woman, it wasn't quite a scarecrow either. In fact, this close he wasn't entirely sure how he saw the thing from his vantage point beneath the tree. He couldn't look away. Keaton felt his soul go cold, his bones suddenly rubbing coarse like sand between china plates. He felt sweat bead on his skin and his breath stumbled and played dead.

It stood nearly seven feet tall. The large wooden T was standard scarecrow fare, but what hung there was anything but. A frayed dress of gossamer and lace, a wedding gown, fluttered in the air. Sun-faded and off white, the front stained dark brown to black in some places. Beneath the gauzy fabric, bones were visible. A ribcage served as a home for whatever was moving in there. Small shadows roiled and seethed. The arms were longer than possible. Twice as long as his. The hands that ended them were scaled and tipped in claw, like large chicken feet. Keaton dropped his gaze and saw that the thing ended below the waist. Long rotted intestines dangled like swamp vines, dried and withered. He licked his quivering lips and looked up once more. Atop the hunched shoulders sat a bovine skull, horns jutted from the sides, long strands of hair were tied to the horns. The left side and most of the bottom were encased in a hornet's nest. Dark gray paper molded around stark bone. The angry bees flew in and out of the eye's sockets. Landing on the carcasses that rimmed the clearing. Keaton looked back at it and heard a whisper. His hand stayed on the pistol at his hip and he watched, unbelievingly, as the skull began to move. The nest covered the lower portion of the skull and Keaton could swear he heard a muffled voice. He took a tentative step back and kept his eye on the thing before him. He saw a small tear begin in the nest's paper and watched as a ragged fissure erupted across the surface of the nest. The skull shook a bit more and a torrent of hornets poured from the new mouth like a venomous tongue. So many that the sky seemed to grow black. Keaton turned and ran. He ran like he never had before. He didn't even turn when he discerned there was crazy laughter that mingled with the buzzing.

JONES

30.

Jones sat on Enterline and watched the sleeping child. He looked around and tried to discern whether there was an adult with him. He was sliding down from the horse when the quiet was shattered by a sudden hollering. Jones stood up straighter and grabbed his gun. He looked around and tried to pinpoint the origin. He moved his gaze from the trees towards the cornfield. Another yell erupted from the corn off to his right. Enterline let out a nervous sound and Jones pulled the lead to stop her from bolting. He half crouched and held his pistol hand out in front. Something was crashing through the drying stalks. Jones felt his hands shake. Felt his palms slick with sweat.

"Hey Mister!" the boy called from over by the tree. He stood in the shade looking disheveled.

Jones glanced and held a finger up to his mouth. He hoped the boy understood the gesture. As he looked back to the field, he saw stalks shaking and heard thundering footfalls. He crouched a little lower and held the gun steady. He hardly had time to blink the perspiration from his eyes before the man burst from the field, white as bone and screaming to beat the band.

The screaming man took in the scene quickly and skidded to a stop. His boot heels gouged grooves in the soft earth. "Hold up, Mister," he urged, palms up and out. Jones stood stock still and just stared at him. His expression of worry and panic began to change, to grow sharp edges and harden. He was familiar with this man. He'd seen his face before. He had ridden with it in his mind and in his guts. He stared and stood straighter and he did not lower the gun. His hand was suddenly quite steady.

KEATON & JONES

31.

"Mister, there is no need for that gun." Keaton said, the words coming in breathy bursts.

"I've not decided on that yet," Jones countered in a cool tone.

"Look, I didn't mean to rattle you screaming like that. I musta looked a sight, shooting out of the corn, howling like a maniac." Keaton leaned forward and tried to slow his breathing.

He held a hand to his side and pushed as he did so. Jones noticed the blood on his boots.

"You hurt?"

"What?" Jones nodded towards his feet and Keaton looked down. The heels and toes slick with gore. "Oh…no. That's from in there."

"What's in there?"

"I don't think I know. An idol, maybe."

"No such thing as an idol."

"I'd be of a mind to agree but weren't another word that seemed to fit what I just saw. Some kind of thing."

Jones took steps toward the corn. The stalks rubbed one another like grasshopper's legs and sang and murmured.

"Don't. Not just yet." Keaton spat into the dirt and watched as the spit began to seep into the ground. The drone from the field began to rise. Keaton looked over his shoulder and saw a funnel of bees rising into the sky. A column of black carapace and whispering wings and deafening buzz.

Jones also stood and stared. The hornets rose until they disappeared into the clouds. There seemed to be millions. He looked to Keaton, who was just as transfixed. From behind Jones came a sound. He heard the boy approaching and stole a side glance to make sure it was no sort of ambush.

The boy stopped and stood. "What's you holdin' on him for?" he asked. Jones wrinkled his nose at the odd carp smell he was picking up. The boy came a little closer and he discovered the odor was coming from the filthy linen he had tied around his shoulder. Something in the sling was moving.

"I'm working it out, son." Jones said. He looked back to the sky. It was clear and gray, as always. He raised an eyebrow at Keaton who just shook his head. He watched Keaton for any sign of attack and saw only a tired and unsettled man, composing himself after being deeply shaken. He slowly slid his gun back in its holster and took a step back in the direction of Enterline, who was happily eating fallen apples from the ground.

"I'm Keaton." He held out a grubby hand and Jones looked at it. How it shook. The black under the nails. Some of that black possibly being ashes from his mother's house. He felt something hot rise in his throat. He made himself swallow it.

"I'm Jones." He took the hand and shook it once then dropped it quick as though it were a dead thing.

Keaton cocked his head a little. "I know you?"

"I don't believe."

"You look a bit familiar to me."

"Maybe you knew my mother." The statement scorched his tongue upon exiting. With it Keaton froze. He made the connection and stood while its icy waters rose over his head. While his air dissipated and fled as mice. This was the old woman's son. As he looked at Jones, the resemblance was uncanny. They had the same nose, same wide eyes. He felt something inside crack and he drew in a deep breath.

"I did know her."

Jones made for his pistol again. Keaton held out a hand. "Not necessary, hear me out." Keaton took a deep breath and looked to Jubal. The boy just gaped at the men before him, his arm holding the bulge of the sling against his side.

"I was ambling and your ma put me up. She stayed me in the barn and I holed up there a week or a few. I can't remember how long. Maybe a month. Time just slithers on. I did chores and helped with fixing fences and livestock. Mended the barn door. Whatever she needed. She paid me in room and food." He saw that his words were doing nothing to dull the sharpness of Jones expression.

"I didn't kill her. That what you're thinking?"

"Did I say she was dead?" Jones scowled and tilted his head sharply, it cracked like a stick.

"She is. That is a fact that I sadly know." Keaton looked at his feet when he spoke. His voice was a feeble and embarrassed thing, cowering naked.

"It's the truth. I know what the law told me. What the poster promised." Jones had his hand on the butt of the gun. "I also know that a promise is often just a longer lie."

"No facts to that. I was there when she was killed. I didn't see who done it. Not clearly. Just that he was big. Timber tall and brazen, and he burned the house down around her. I tried to put it out." Keaton was starting to cry. He was back in that night now. "I saw the man getting away and I went after him. I figured the townsfolk would pin it on me. The tall man just big stepped right outta that valley. Singing as he did so." He stopped and composed himself. "I give you my word, I never touched that woman." Jones allowed his hand to fall to his side. He had listened as Bob Ford had urged him to, with his heart as well as his ears and he had heard the truth. He exhaled loudly through his nose.

"I believe you." Jones paused and slid his gun back into its holster. He looked at Keaton for a long few minutes, "I will say that you are very lucky. Lucky we did not cross paths a month ago." He stood a while longer, then turned and began to walk back to his horse. Keaton watched the man tether his horse and then walk back to where he and the boy stood.

"Grief is a hungry fuel. And it will devour anything to keep burning. I had been gunning for you, and had every intention of erasing you from the world." Jones kicked an apple and watched the bruised flesh split and the worms beneath turn.

"Changed your heart?" Jubal pressed as he adjusted his sling. One of the sisters let out a low mewling sound. Jones furrowed his brow and Keaton shook his head. Jones took his meaning and kept on like he'd seen or heard nothing. He looked at the kid, "I met a man who taught me plenty. I'll leave it at that."

"Always room for learnin'. My ma always said that." Jubal offered. Jones smiled and nodded at the boy and then met the gaze of Keaton.

"Where are you two aimed?"

"We were headed for anywhere that'd have us. But nearly every town we've passed by is dead. Burnt to the ground. Farms all gone to rot. Truth be, you're the first living soul we've seen since Tiny last week." Keaton scratched at his bearded face.

"I heard as much. There is a murderer afoot. Killing towns." Jones leaned against the tree and slowly slid to a sitting position.

"Who told you that?"

"A wolf." Jones answered. Keaton opened his mouth to say something but thought better of it, as the words sluiced into his mouth he realized that nothing seemed unreasonable anymore.

"How could someone kill an entire town?" Jubal asked.

"Well, they're all small. You slink in and start at one end, I reckon you'd get pretty near the other end before anyone caught on. Especially if you were quiet about things." Keaton added.

"And if you were fearful enough, even after they caught on." Jones nodded.

"I suspect you could come along with us, Mister Jones." Jubal offered, looking to Keaton after the fact. Keaton added nothing.

"Maybe for a ways. Maybe as far as Lansdale."

"What's there?" Keaton looked up again. Behind the tree, the sun was falling behind the ridge.

"Nothing. Just a start, maybe."

"Sounds like as good a place as any." Keaton took a step towards the tree and leaned against the trunk. He took out his pouch and began to roll a smoke. He offered the leather to Jones, who politely refused.

"You have no horse?" Jones asked as he looked around.

"I had one. Upon a time. It was before I was amblin'." He paused and licked the paper gluing it with his spit. "I was younger than now, at least by a year or three," he paused and smiled. "I fancied myself a gunslinger. Had me a nice gun and a showy belt. Left my home to find my fame and fortune. Shit lasted maybe a month before I found out."

"Found out what?"

"That what you want and what you need is nary the same thing."

"Sometimes to know you are well, something has to come along and hurt you." Jones said, nodding.

"Pretty much. I fell in with some guys and thought they'd show me the outlaw ropes. But they showed me ropes alright. Tied me in knots inside I still ain't undone." Keaton began to speak slower and stare off into the corn. He was getting lost again.

"Your horse?" Jones pressed.

"Them fuckers drank her." He looked up, a lop-sided smile on his face. "We were without water for days and so they shot her and drank her." Keaton put his hands over his face and the noise that came from behind them was almost a growl. "I waited until they bedded down, and I snuck off. I wandered for nearly three more days before I made it to Lut's Key. And then met your Ma. She saved me. And I couldn't even return the favor."

"It's done. Things behind are just that. You only move on by looking forward. "

"He's a good man, Mr. Jones. He took me on. And I ain't nothing to him," Jubal said.

"You're something, son. I suspect by saving you, Keaton was saving himself." Jones stole another glance at Keaton and saw that he was getting it together. "Show me this idol of yours." Jones unsnapped his holster again. Keaton nodded and stood up, the bark rasped against his vest as he rose.

"You stay here, Kid," he said, and Jubal frowned. "You gotta protect your sisters." At that Jubal nodded and puffed out his young chest, his dirty hands curling into fists.

Jones nodded, and the two men made their way into the corn. Behind them, the boy whispered into the cotton folds of the sling.

JUBAL, KEATON & JONES

32.

The sun had burned black and matched the sky now. There was no visible moon but the stars were bright and gave off a surreal glimmer. The two men hadn't said much since returning from the cornfield. The color was finally returning to Jones's face. He had stopped trembling. Keaton just shook his head every so often and released an uneasy titter of a laugh. Several times Jones opened his mouth as if to speak, to address the thing in the corn, but his eyes would twitch and he'd draw a deep breath and clamp his mouth closed to trap it inside. The flames into which they stared just crackled.

The night was cooling fast and the fire they'd made gave off a comfortable warmth. Jones sat nearest the flames and held the apple over them. He'd made a slit in its skin and was watching for the juices to begin to bubble from it like a wound as it heated. Keaton just kept an eye on the field and smoked another cigarette.

"What was out there?" Jubal finally asked. He tossed his apple core over for Enterline to eat, and she did just that. Keaton remained silent. A breeze picked up and rustled the stalks in the field. It sounded like voices.

"A monster." Jones muttered, "An honest-to-God monster."

"My Ma said there ain't no such thing as monsters."

Jones smiled. "There's often nothing but monsters. Monsters are different things to different people, son."

Keaton was speaking now: "What is a monster to you might be an angel to me or a demon to him. Everything is the same and different to everyone and no one."

Jones smiled as it occurred to him that this stranger he had just met had perhaps uttered the most Bob Fordian statement he'd heard since his friend passed on. The fire shimmied and the boy yawned, "Why don't you bed down, Kid. We'll start out again at light."

Jubal smiled and nodded at Keaton. "I am a bit tired."

Jubal lifted the sling over his head and laid it on the ground.

He adjusted his shirt but not before both men saw the dark bruises that lined his side, dark purple areas, rimmed in yellow and jeweled with scabs. The men exchanged looks and both just looked away as Jubal put the sling back on and turned with his face to the trunk of the tree. From inside the folds came a chittering clicking sound followed by what sounded like moist whispers that the boy answered in a small voice. All the sounds soon became one with the sounds of the boy's snoring.

The two men sat in silence and the night was just that, until the howl of a wolf worked its fingers into the seams. After that the men began to talk low.

LEVI

33.

His lips still slick with the grease from the charred flesh he had eaten, Levi smiled up at the stars. They winked and whispered to him. He felt his skin dancing for them. His blood sang. He looked at his arms, the nails he had pulled from the fingers of the miners at the first camp he'd erased in even rows up his forearms. They shimmered like scales in the fickle light. He sat and gnawed at the last of the meat and crisped fat, then tossed the leg and attached foot into the brush. Something startled and fled deeper into the weeds and overgrowth. He still held the little shoe in his other hand. Brown leather scuffed at the toes. His nostrils flared as he took in the faint tang of young sweat from it. He laughed and threw it into the weeds as well. He reached down and picked up two arms from the pile of limbs he had assembled after the school fire burned out. He looked at the hands and smiled, it was nothing but teeth. He hunched forward and pulled his knife from his back pocket, flicking out the blade as he reached back around. He went to work liberating the middle fingers from the hands.

"If you call me, call me Devil," he sang as he took the digits and held them against the thick flesh of his forehead. He felt nothing as the flesh reached out and swallowed the stumps of the fingers. Centered between them, smack in the middle of his forehead was the birthmark he'd taken from the doctor woman. He looked at himself in the dark surface of the pond, and though rippled by the breeze, he could see his newly acquired horns. "If you call me Devil, then here I am," he crooned in a deep voice and the fingers began to twitch and waggle. Levi laughed and stood up from where he had rested. He picked up his hat and sat it on his mangy head, further back than usual. The middle fingers hooked themselves over the brim and held it in place as he took the night in big strides. Cavern-deep inside of him, the shreds of old Levi— the untouched Levi—were screaming at the things he'd done, was doing, would do. It was a whisper in a windstorm. Somewhere above, an owl called and when it received no reply, it simply sat silent and watched as a monster trudged off into the night.

KEATON & JONES & JUBAL

34.

"She's mourning." Jones spoke after the wolf howled another time or two, seeming quite close. Keaton held his gun and looked into the darkness. Jones shook his head. "Nothing to fear. She's a widow. She will be no danger to us. She's been shadowing me for days."

"Like a guardian angel?" Keaton chided and slid the pistol back in its place.

"I collect those." Jones replied and Keaton either ignored the remark or plain didn't get it. Jones dropped the core of his apple into the fire and cocked his head. "I was fortunate, that while I was making my way to you, I met a wonderful man who taught me some things. Just fresh ways to see old sights. Fresh tongue to old sour milk."

"This that fella Ford you mention?"

"Yes. The wolf we heard is his widow."

"What?"

"You heard me. She follows us close but far."

Keaton yawned so wide it seemed to halve his face. "What happened to him?"

Jones just nodded and the smile he'd been wearing melted and curled into a sad sort of frown. "He was eaten alive."

"A mountain lion or bear?" Keaton sat up a little as he asked.

"A coal mine. Swallowed him a wheeze at a time." Keaton made a sorry face and shook his head. "I'm sorry about your friend."

The fire was dwindling but the cool of the night hadn't

grown any, the men allowed the feeble light to dance over their tired features. They had spent the first hour or so after Jubal fell asleep, telling one another of their lives, select bites that seemed tasty and easy to swallow. They both sat on the tree side of the fire, keeping the cornfield in view at all times. Their glances into the wheezing stalks was nearly feral at times. Jones kept his gun on his thigh while Keaton held his in a shaking hand.

Jones looked at Keaton and felt a twinge of shame at the hate he had tried to harbor for this man. This stranger who was navigating the same soulful impasse as he. In another time and place, they could have been brothers.

"Jubal and me was making our way East from where I found him. We passed through a spatter of little villages—Gabino, Maryville, Ripple and Noonan. Some weren't even villages just a handful of houses planted and grown together in a bunch." He paused to take a drag from his cigarette. "We camped the night on the edge of the property I was born on, was raised up on. I never told the boy I was heading home but I felt a pull and needed— wanted to see my Pa again." In the air above them, wings flapped and something squalled.

"Was he glad to see you?" Jones ventured, knowing from the look on the man's face that would not be the outcome.

"He was gone. All that marked the fact he…we ever were there was the weeded over stones from the foundation and a few timbers that stuck up like bones. The barn had been burned. His anvil still sat on the stump but was rusted and grown up with vines." Another drag and he allowed the smoke to escape from his flaring nostrils. "There was no one around. My heart hurt to see it but at first I assumed they'd moved on for some reason."

Jones watched as the man worked through the riddles behind his eyes.

"I waited until Jubal was asleep that night. We had a fat moon, bright as blazes. I took a walk and that's when I found it. Over behind where the house had stood, was a tree. When I was little it was a rope swing tree. A weeping willow. It was the only thing that seemed to be thriving in that valley. The viney branches still lush and green. It looked odd to me, so I walked closer and then I lit a match. It burned out quickly, so I took out my handkerchief and tied it around the end of a stick, then I lit another and set it aflame. I held it out and saw that hanging among those low branches were bones. I saw that they were whole skeletons. I saw the one that's legs dragged on the ground, the one that's bones ended below the knees was wearing faded and torn overalls. His smithin' gloves was still in the pocket…" Keaton left his words trail off and he sat and stared into the fire that was growing slight.

"Did you get to say goodbye?" Jones' voice was a cold drink in scorching heat, "A farewell is both an opening and closing door."

"I did. Once I was done crying and saying sorry. I told him he was right and that I weren't nothing but a spoiled and stupid kid. But that now I was a stupid and anxious man. Wearing the yoke of all my trespasses. I figured him to be sneering at me from above." Keaton paused again before he went on. "I think they was killed by the same man—thing—what killed your mama. Who's been taking out towns across the land." Keaton flicked the rest of his smoke into the fire and it jumped lively for a second.

"A man like that can no longer be a man. A man who has done a thing like kill without reason and has felt it grow and grow, he's not likely to be a man at all anymore. A man what starts on a trail such as this, it's my thinking he may not have been much of a man to begin with."

"Maybe he never got the chance to be. Maybe he was made a monster before he was grown?" Keaton was rambling. Jones took a small nibble from his ninth apple and rolled the rest over to his horse. Enterline took it all in a single bite.

"We need some rest. Tomorrow, we'll head towards Lansdale. Maybe we can find some people to help us find this monster and we can put a stop to his path." Jones spoke with eyes barely open.

"Or maybe we can close our eyes and smother in the webs of sleep and never wake again." Keaton intoned, and Jones was unnerved that there was no trace of smile or snark. He said no more, just untied his hair and sat his hat over his eyes and within minutes they were all three snoring. The fire muttered and chanted of warmth and smoke.

LEVI

35.

He was having one of them moments. The kind what came with more and more infrequency since he lit out a few years ago. A miniscule lull in a heavy rainstorm. The chorus of whispers in his head dulled and he was allowed to think for himself and recall. The strings were still there but the flitting and gnarled old hands that pulled and yanked them to make him dance were momentarily still. He remembered his Pa, tucking him in and telling him of the strangeness of their land. The dark history of it. A history writ in dust and dirt and stone and blood. Spoken on the wind and rain and in shadow speak and spider skulk. He recalled that he had told him it was shunned land by the Indians and by whomever had lived here before them. It was a desolate place and therefore his kin had gotten it for nothing. If they were fool enough to want it. The tribes called it a "Thin-Skinned place." Not long after, his grandpap had built the farm and handed it down from son to son to son. They still called it a farm though the ground yielded nothing but fat pulsating grubs and malformed vegetables that tasted like salt and smoke. But it was a place to live. Levi smiled a sad smile as he saw his Pa in his mind's bloodshot eye. He could see the small wrinkles around his eyes and hear that deep throaty voice that spoke so calmly to him so long ago. He could feel the callus of his thumb as he stroked his temple as he tucked him in bed. *"Goodnight, Son."*

His pa had succumbed to the fever and Levi was left in the care of his grandfather. A wickedly stern man with little patience and a littler heart. It is at this juncture in his memory where things go off the rails. He sees himself at the rain barrel. Sees himself looking up at himself. He can see long shadows underground, like big fish sliding through cloudy waters. Movement in the skies behind the clouds, enormous things that writhe and flex behind the thick fog. He sees a hole in the sky where the monsters leak in. He sees a large and hideous man fighting with two others. He sees it all in blaring red. He once again refreshes himself with the duty at hand. He is a carpenter. He is the builder of the door. It's taken years of growth and blood to paint the mural of his life, of his destiny. He feels cold itching behind his watering eyes. "Please, just a few more minutes, please…"

    The voices start up again. Promises and wagers. Directions and epiphanies. Instructions and insanities. He always feels the pull. He is a magnet and they are steel filings. They dance for each other before they take one another. Levi gasps as the image of the outcome burns into his fevered brain. The beauty is a scorching thing. He begins to shift his bulk from where it sits. The night and the darkness have their hooks in him, by Gods. A throaty laugh jumps from his mouth. Levi stands and looks down at his feet. His boots had worn through so long ago that the bottoms of his feet had no flesh left. The meat has long evacuated and left bone and dirt crusted tissues as the sole. Levi stretches and feels his skin slide, his bones pop like kindling. He takes a step and closes his eyes. He can feel the way he is to go. The path he is to walk. His purpose has made him a divining rod. He looks up at the moon and smiles, he ejaculates and feels it, thick and curdled, on his blistered thigh. From above the pale light catches all of those teeth and twinkles like stars. Levi walked on and on and on.

BUZZARD

36.

The morning sun was a boil on pale skin. Angry and bloated with pus. The carrion bird flew higher and circled over the land. The smoking ruins of towns and the rotting corpse piles around them drew him like a flirtatious wink courts a lonely man. It was like a battlefield, and the bird was quite familiar with those. Had it been able to process what it saw, it would have noted that the carcasses of the villages and towns and the carnage scattered between—the smoldering skeletons and wasted structures— formed a line. And that one line touched another. That when looked at from above as a complete picture, they formed a diamondesque shape. It was like looking down at a map. Were it able to communicate in a language comparable, it would have told of the mannish thing. The giant that was behind it all. The behemoth that shambled from the end of the shape towards the town nestled in its center. The broken stinger in the center of the swollen sting. Of how the edges of the perimeter looked like the puffy and infected lips of a wound. How smoke was seeping from the edges. The buzzard circled and flattened its wings to glide further and further out. When it got closer, close enough to fly directly over the southern-most edge of the diamond, it stopped. Exploding with a hard crack as it slid down the sky and fell to the ground below. Bloody feathers, bulging eyes and a cracked beak. Blood slowly trickled down from the splatter on the unseen wall that marked the bottom edge of the diamond. The blood began to disappear, and the sound of lapping tongues broke the silence.

The air filled with ecstatic groans. Shadows flickered behind the clouds. Below, on the scorched ground, the remains of the buzzard were still. The dust drank its leaking blood like man dying of thirst.

JONES

37.

Keaton and Jubal were still sleeping. Their snoring reminded Jones of the hogs his father had at one time. Loathsome creatures, mean and smelly. His Pa had gotten rid of them after the boar had bitten off his left thumb. *Gotten rid of* meant he had split its skull with a hammer and hung it in the barn to bleed dry. Then as a final insult to that nasty creature, they ate him all winter long. He smiled at the memory of his pa and smoked ham and took a few steps towards the corn. He pulled his gun and held it in a sweaty hand and stole another glance back at his new friends. Seeing that they still slept, he entered the field. He snuck a hand into his shirt and rubbed the lump by his heart. He could feel his heartbeat there. He felt a little stronger and a lot more scared.

He stepped from the stalks into the clearing and stopped dead in his tracks. The gun made a *thunk* as it hit the dirt. The carcasses were all gone. Every last one of them. The ground was still dark with congealed blood and flies the size of hummingbirds danced around lazily. He looked to the spot where the scarecrow stood, and it was still there. The hornet's nest was still smothering the cow skull. The tear where the torrent of bees had flown from the day before was still a ragged paper mouth. Only now, it was smeared with thick blood. At the base of the wooden stake upon which it hung, was a large pile of bones. Picked clean and glistening in the morning light. He slowly knelt and retrieved his weapon, his eyes never leaving the thing on the post. Was its head turned? It didn't move, did it? He stared at the thing. The blood that stained the already dirty muslin. The ribs beneath. But it was the distended globe beneath those ribs that troubled him. The pregnant bloat that pulsed and twisted beneath the frayed fabric. The muted mewling that he swore he could almost hear. He was suddenly drenched in sweat as he started the step backwards into the corn. He looked up at the skull once more and for an instant he saw his mother's face staring down at him. Large eyes lined with disapproval and scorn. Her stare bore into him and his mouth went desert dry. Then she opened her mouth and he heard a buzzing. Saw the wings of her tongue and imagined the stingers. And underneath that he heard an infant's wail. A hungry and needy sound.

He bolted into the rows. Turning and running full speed once he was out of sight of the thing. His boot heels sinking in the rancid mud. He could have sworn he heard screams mixing with those other vile sounds until he realized they were his own.

KEATON

38.

Keaton was flat on his back in the field. The sky above him was framed in smoky pillars that rose from the rubble around him. His arms were spread out away from him. In each of his hands sat one of Jubal's sisters. They had their eyes open. He squinted into the dull brightness of the sky. Birds fell like dark falling stars. The sky was teaming with shadows. Large and long and slithering behind clouds, behind the fabric of sky itself. He heard thunder rumble. It reminded him of a starving man's stomach. He turned his head and watched the flames lick at the air from the dying buildings. Arms jutting from piles of brick and sizzling timber. He heard another roll of thunder and looked back to the sky when the bolt of lightning split it off to the left a little. He watched the sky bleed, thick ropes of red raining from the laceration. He caught a glimpse of what was making the shadows and he opened his mouth to scream. He screamed so hard his guts trembled and his bowels let loose. He felt something coarse in his chest, he coughed and screamed at the same time, the volume of his shrieks becoming a rasping howl. The flourish of hornets that blew from his lips rose to the new doorway in the sky and swarmed the unfathomable face of the God peeking through.

KEATON & JONES

39.

Keaton opened his eyes. He was under the tree, next to Jubal who still snored into his arm. He sat up and wiped the thick sheen of sweat from his face. He couldn't stop shaking. He looked down at the large wet spot on the front of his pants. From the smell there was more mess on the back. He slowly stood and steadied himself against the trunk of the tree and looked over at Enterline who just stared back, harboring no judgment for the man who had soiled himself in his sleep. Keaton looked to where the fire had been, where the stone-rimmed ashes smoldered. Jones was gone. He was just about to go find somewhere to rinse his pants and then wake the boy when the screaming started. He jumped to his feet and swiveled towards the corn. "Good thing I already messed 'em," he muttered as he grabbed for his gun. The rows rustled as something big tore through them. Keaton pulled up the gun and stood ready, scared as hell but ready.

Jones burst from the field like a cannonball. He stopped the instant he saw the man with the piss-stain on his crotch and the gun in his hand aimed right at him.

"Hold it!" He exclaimed with his hands up, his own gun hanging from the thumb of his right hand.

"Christ, Man! You have any idea how close you come?" Keaton slid his gun back in the holster and leaned forward to draw deeper breaths. They tasted of piss.

"Sorry I scared you so much." Jones started to laugh. An uneasy titter.

Keaton looked at him and saw he was looking at his pants. "Don't flatter yourself. I'd already pissed and shit myself before you came along and scared me." Jones shook his head and pointed into the corn.

"I went to see the scarecrow. The animals are gone now. There are bones around it. It's pregnant and vile." Jones spoke with a calm manner that unsettled Keaton.

"I was dreaming." Keaton paused and licked his lips. They were bleeding where he must've bitten himself. "I was laying in this field and looking up to the sky. The sky broke and there were things behind it. Awesome and monstrous. I screamed until I screamed up bees. I pissed myself, shit myself too. That was in the dream and then I woke up to it in real life." Keaton then giggled himself. He worried a little that the two of them might be losing their minds.

"I have an extra pair of dungarees in my bag. They ought to..." Jones paused to look Keaton over. "Actually probably be a little short. Bob Ford was a tall man in many ways with height not being one of them." The two chuckled and walked towards where Enterline stood eating some grass.

"That was a terrifying dream." Keaton muttered as Jones rifled through his bag.

"Mine too. But it was no dream."

"Let me change into them pants and we'll go back in together and check it out, while Jubal is still sleeping."

"Wash yourself first. No sense putting clean pants on if you stay filthy."

Keaton stopped and pondered that for a second or two. He shook his head and realized that he would have done just that. He walked over to the fire ring and tapped the kettle and found it still pretty warm. He dumped the water on the leg of his rancid pants and then set about wiping himself. Jones looked away out of respect.

"I think I saw what I saw and you dreamed what you dreamed for a reason. I think we're being given an invitation." Jones paused and thought more on his words. "Not an invitation but more like an interception. Like a traitor would be intercepting secret plans. We're being shown what is coming and hints at how to stop it."

"I never saw any such indication of stopping it." Keaton grunted and shook his head, forcing his foot into the leg of the denim jeans. As he buttoned them, he noted that they stopped about an inch and half above his ankle. He smirked and tucked them into his boots. "Actually, it sort of reminds me of them webs. The kind those spiders make that look like funnels. They build 'em in the corners of barns in dark spots and it tricks their prey into going right to 'em."

"That is not a comforting concept." Jones noted.

"I didn't think so either, I'm hoping that comes next." They laughed again out of tension and then as soon as Keaton had buttoned his front, they headed off into the cornfield yet again. Enterline stood and watched them disappear into the stalks.

KEATON & JONES

40.

Just as Jones had promised, the scarecrow was gone. The wooden frame that had been its perch still stood, the base surrounded by mounds of bones. The bones were dusted with dead hornets. Jones tapped a small pile with the toe of his boot. Nothing moved. The husks of dead bees crunched under their every step. Keaton looked warily around the clearing.

"I'm thinking this is what the old timers would refer to as a portent." Jones offered.

"I have no idea what that means." Keaton admitted.

"Just a fancy way of saying it was a hint. A horrible hint that tells us something terrible is coming."

"I think I could've sussed that without the ugly scarecrow and shitting my pants, thank you."

The earth was still darkened with the blood of the slain animals, but they were gone now. Like the hellish scarecrow that had held court here. That damned thing that Jones swore had eaten the carcasses and was pregnant with something evil was nowhere in sight. Jones was tipping the mounds of bones, looking for something that was a mystery to him when he let out a small gasp. Keaton stopped moving and went to where his new friend stood. Jones nodded down the pile of small vertebrae he had pushed aside. There was an odd bone laying on the blackened soil. It looked like a rib. There were grooves in it where it had been gnawed. Some deeper than others. A hole had been bored through one of the ends. Keaton stared at it for a full minute before he got it.

"My God. It's a damned key," he nearly shouted as he looked into the damp face of Jones.

"I fear that is exactly what it looks like." Jones bent and picked it up. It felt warm in his hands and as he slid it into the inside pocket of his vest he swore he felt it vibrate against the skin. Against the lump of metal that lived beneath it. It made him think of a tuning fork.

Keaton stared at the hole in the damp ground where the key had been. At the dried worms that lined the spot. "I feel like a stranger anymore. Not knowing where I am or where I'm going."

"I've always felt as such. Oddly, I'm starting to feel a little more comfortable now that the world has caught on to it." Jones tried to chuckle but it was a deformed thing that limped away.

"Let's go back and wake the kid and get the hell out of here."

"Let's do just that." Jones walked into the corn and Keaton walked behind him, backwards so he could keep an eye on the clearing until the cornstalks swallowed them and obscured it from view.

KEATON, JONES & JUBAL

41.

"A key ain't always like the kind you stick in a lock. Sometimes it's just an answer." Keaton said as he looked at the strange carved bone they had found in the clearing.

"Maybe this is both. But maybe it ain't either." Jubal offered as he scratched his head, his thick and dirty hair hardly moved. He chewed the dandruff from under his nails. "Can't be a key if there ain't no keyhole."

"A key can be an explanation. A savior. Or a thing that locks the chains that keep you down." Jones added.

"We need a damned key to the key." Keaton laughed but it was a nervous sound. Loud and wavery. He held the key between shaking fingers. Jones was glad to be rid of it for the time being. It had made him feel strange and uncomfortable.

"So, you found that in the field with the idol? I wish I'd have gotten to see that thing. Why'd you fellas let me sleep?" Jubal sounded indignant.

The men kept examining the key and ignored his whining interjections. Jubal shifted his sling and it elicited some muted clicking sounds. Like chattering teeth. Jones looked at the boy who was looking down into the dirty folds of linen. He heard the boy speaking very softly. He held the bulging part close to his side and hissed through his teeth, a wince taking over his face for a brief moment. Jones looked away for a minute and felt like he ought to just run like hell. Then he remembered that hell has a way of following a man. Hell is as close as your own damn heart, Hell and home are both four-letters long, but one is forever while the other is easily gone.

They walked slowly for a while before the wind picked up and they caught a whiff of rain on it. They hastened their pace until they reached the edge of Butler-Ferguson, or what had been the town(s) until recently. They stopped, the three of them and just surveyed the devastation. Every building had been leveled by fire. Blackened brace logs and timbers jutted out at odd angles. Bits of metal and melted globs of glass littered the street. And scattered around all of that were so many bones. They looked like seashells on a filthy beach. A snakeskin boot lay in the middle of the street. It was teeming with flies.

Jubal bent and picked up something silver from the ground. He held it up and showed it to Jones. "Gold!" the boy exclaimed.

"That's a tooth. Just drop it." The man winced. The boy did as he was told and walked on. Keaton was reminded of the war and how it ate up so many villages and men. Not caring much for who was on what side. Hunger is hunger and war is a voracious thing. Whatever tore through here had a similar appetite. He stole a glance at Jones who was wearing a twin expression. A large bird flew from what was left of the saloon. It was mineshaft black and shined like tar. The men and the boy kept moving. There were small noises from within the rubble. Scuttling sounds and whispers molded from mud and mildew. They made their way through the corpse of a town and hoped they could make it to Fallon by dusk. Jones just hoped there was a Fallon to make it to.

LEVI

42.

The man walked slower now. Much slower. He had found that he wasn't as mean as he had been nearer the beginning. He'd had the shadows living within him for years now. At least it felt like much longer. Time no longer mattered, it was just a thing that twisted and coiled like roots or guts. The anger and rage that his tenants had raised within him had settled. The barbs and stings of their incessant ranting and screeching had dulled and he no longer felt them. He still killed and committed their horrible bidding, but he really just wanted this to be over. He was still ready to do what he had to, but the promised release was the prize at the end of the race for him. He stooped and hobbled a few more steps. His bones were changing. He was changing. Any resemblance to the farm boy he started life as had been long obliterated. He was a giant of welt red and sharp bone. His flesh was scaled with fingernails and he had fingers growing from his forehead. Ears down the side of his neck that pulsed like gills. His skin was a patchwork of pieces from everyone he'd killed. A quilted monster. The voices stopped speaking, sort of. They wailed and screeched in unison, a throbbing siren behind his eyes that never ceased. He stomped heavier upon the ground, the instant when his heavy foot hit the dry dirt, that thud, allowed him a millisecond of peace as it drowned out the din. His ragged breath wheezed and bubbled from the ruins of his mouth, so crammed with teeth that it was like some ancient draw bridge made of pointed bones. Ropes of drool and blood slicked his neck and chest. He continued walking, following the invisible tether that guided him, like a leash. He looked up to the grey sky and tears wet his cheeks. Deep down, in the tiny island that was still him, down beneath the coal black crust that cocooned his heart, he longed to break the lead and run. Back to the way it was before. Something in the hills howled at the moon, a deep and mournful sound, and so Levi opened his mouth, wider than natural and howled back. It echoed for miles and miles.

JONES & KEATON & JUBAL

43.

"I gotta make water," Jubal announced as they slowed just outside of Fallon. "Can you hold this?" Jubal asked as he lifted the sling over his head and walked towards Keaton. The man didn't bother to hide the grimace that strode across his face, he just held out his arm. The boy hung the sling over his forearm and dashed off into the darkness along the woods.

"I swear to God this thing is heavier." Keaton mumbled to Jones who, stepped a little closer.

Jones took out a match and struck it and Keaton pulled the dirty folds of linen open. His eyes bulged as he noted that the bigger thing...the big sister was bigger now. Easily the size of a grapefruit. Its hair was thick and matted and that cleft mouthful of teeth was rimmed in scabbed blood. The smaller sister was unchanged in appearance, just looked a lot smaller now. Like an apple left to dry in the sun. It throbbed, like the sides of a cat when it sleeps.

"The bigger one has grown." Keaton half-whispered as Jones held the match lower and closer. They saw a small indentation above the toothsome orifice of the larger sister. Beneath it something pulsed. Jones felt the heat on his fingers from the match nearing its end when the sister opened her bright blue eye. Keaton yelped and dropped the sling into the dirt. The two men just stared at the bundle of cloth with those things in its folds as it lay in the road. Filthy as it was, the linen seemed to glow in the moonlight. They heard branches snapping and weeds being trampled and knew Jubal was coming back. Keaton bent and picked up the sling. He held it as far away from himself as he could. Jones looked at it and at the boy who was ambling out of the night.

"Take your kin so we can go." Jones spoke, and it was a stark and rough-edged tone he used. Jubal pulled the sling over his head and adjusted it. He cradled the bulge against his side and a smooth purr rose from the folds. They all kept walking, and no one spoke.

JUBAL & JONES

44.

The fire gave off little warmth but much light in the closeness of the evening. The sky bled darker and darker. The absence of stars was unsettling. Jones swigged the last of his coffee and refilled the tin cup. He looked over at Keaton who was sound asleep against the fallen tree. His soft snores somehow reassuring.

"I'm sorry about your Ma." Jubal spoke, and it cracked the quiet air that had surrounded them.

"Thank you. I'm sorry about yours as well." Jones raised his cup and Jubal did the same. His held only water as he wasn't able to tolerate the taste of burnt coffee yet.

"She was a good woman." Jubal cocked his head and the flames danced in the threat of tears in his eyes. "She taught me so much. She was teachin' me even when she didn't know it. I learned a lot by accident. Lessons that just kinda floated around her and landed on me." At this, the boy smiled but it was a sad one. Jones nodded and took a bite of the apple he held in his other hand.

"Jubal. Those are the most important lessons. The ones taught outright, are just that. Expected. But those that just kind of happen are the ones that will stick and have much greater importance on these rags we call lives."

"Your ma teach you like that?"

Jones considered this, his expression icing over slightly. "Not quite," he paused. "She did at one time but then my father died and with him most of her. Her kindness seemed to hobble and needed put down. Her heart shivered, and her words grew sharp and stony. She never hurt me, outwardly. Just faded to a shadow of the woman that bore me." He took a drink of his coffee and swished it around his mouth, as if to drown the words he was thinking. "Yes. My mother died when my father did. She just wasn't aware of the fact."

"My pa sounds a lot like your ma. A little 'ceptin' my pa drank himself to dead inside. Then even as he tried he couldn't get to livin' again. Not really." He sipped his water and went on. "I kinda think that when my Ma died, he was happy. Maybe not happy but he felt like he was free and so he went about setting himself as free as he possibly could." The boy stopped speaking and Jones felt his brow furrow as he processed what Jubal was getting at. This child was a boy no longer. Most likely hadn't been since the day he saw his father cut those things from his mother's womb.

"I think you're right. A man can never be truly free as long as there is air in his lungs to hold him down." Jones gulped the dregs of his coffee and sat the cup upside down on one of the stones that ringed the fire.

"I'm going to sleep. We want to start early."

"Okay. Goodnight, Mr. Jones." Jubal offered as he wriggled down into his blanket.

"Stephen," the man all but whispered.

"What?"

"My name is Stephen." With that the tired man closed his eyes and listened as the fire crackled and the other man snored and the little boy who was a man inside hummed a lullaby into the folds of that rancid sling. The sky was fish eye glassy, cinder black and still starless.

KEATON & JONES & JUBAL

45.

The next morning things had become quite different. The road grew narrow as though the woods and high growth were trying to choke it out altogether. The trees were all blighted and leprous, bowing over the earth and mourning themselves. Covered in thick white fungus and damp clots of moss like a drowned woman's hair. The air was empty of sound. The silence felt heavy. No birdsong, no rustle of leaf or cracking of branch. Not even a faint breeze. Just stillness and eerie quiet, save for the crunch of stone and dirt beneath worn boots. Keaton stopped and held a hand over his eyes, peering at the distance through the wavery heat that was already rising from the baked ground. The horizon looked oddly hazy, like looking through a window fogged by condensation. He dropped his hand back to his side and resumed his pace. Jones followed with Enterline's lead in his hand. Atop the horse, Jubal still slept, his arms around the horse's neck and the sling hanging down over one flank, bouncing slightly.

"I see some smoke up a ways. Probably miles, at least another day of walking. Hard to be certain, it's mighty hazy." Keaton spoke between huffing breaths.

"That would be what? Haddon?" Jones asked as he tried to run down the list of dead towns they'd passed through in the last few days.

"Nah. Haddon was yesterday. After Fallon. I think that one is Yates. Which is the last little town before we come to Lansdale." Keaton stopped and leaned on his knees, breathing hard. Jones stopped behind him and the horse as well.

"I've never been this far East." Jones admitted. He sipped from the canteen before handing it over to the other man. The water's cool metallic tang felt good on his lips.

"I was in Yates once. Nothing but a drunkard's den. Ain't nothing but a tavern and a whorehouse hotel. Just a place for miners and cowhands to drink and fuck for the night." Keaton took a gulp and swallowed it loudly. He stoppered the canteen and handed it back.

"Let's keep at it." Keaton started up again and Jones followed suit. The air gripped them like a clammy hand and squeezed.

LEVI

46.

Lansdale had proven a bitch to kill but he'd done it. He had started at the southern end and strangled the boy who was minding the stable. It took one hand and hardly any effort and his neck snapped like kindling. He set the hay ablaze and was through the mercantile, the sheriff's office and blacksmith's before the flames migrated to the saloon. No one tried to stop him, by this stage of his appearance, they never did. Most seemed to turn to stone as though he were Medusa. Frozen solid until they burned.

The town was the final edge to the door he was building. The instructions that whizzed and bit inside his brain for these last months were now nearly carried out. He stood, and his labored breaths practically dripped from his shredded and swollen lips. He had even cast the line for the key. Yanked and set the hook. The men and boy ought to arrive any time now with it. Levi tried to smile, the pieces of lip scabbed to his cheek pulled uncomfortably. He looked to the sky and the shadows that swam behind the clouds. "The door is done!" he shouted. "Theeorrishunnnn!" is what people actually would have heard him bellow. Blood and spit flecking his chin with every mushed word. He wiped it with his sleeve and gripped his lips with trembling fingers and pulled them free. He ate them quickly and without chewing. "Done," he spoke again, clearer. He walked to center of the street. Along either side, buildings smoked and wood still sizzled as it cooled. The smoke whirled in small funnels and chased itself around the corpses that lined the destruction. Levi looked up to the clouds once more and tears began to escape from his milky eyes. He understood that the anger that rooted in his core was his. It began as grief when his father died and then the seeds of that grief tangled with those of anger and hate sown by his grandfather. By the time the things that dwelled beneath the property came calling—the things that flitted in shadowy lofts and crawled beneath timber floors. Those what scuttled under brush and beneath root. Those things had burrowed inside of him and got down deep. They took and ate those seeds and vomited up a black ichor that was all he seemed to be now. He had thoughts still his, once in a rare while they allowed him those. He found that he was a top winding down from all the spinning. There was no string to wrap around and give the yank to restart him. He was weary and in agony and ready for it to be over. There was a loud crash behind him. The roof on the livery fell in. Somewhere in the smoke and orange glow, a baby was wailing. The sound made him salivate. He was so tired, and this. This was almost finished. Maybe then he could rest. Maybe then he could just be a man again. Levi wished he could recall what hope was like.

KEATON & JONES & JUBAL

47.

"Hold up." Keaton stopped and held a hand up to Jones and the boy. Jones made a noise and the horse stopped.

"What's happening?" Jubal asked, sleepily as he sat up and rubbed his cheek, reddened from where it had been resting against Enterline. No one answered. Keaton took a few more steps and stopped. He pointed towards the forest on their right. The dark green of the evergreens and the shadowy trunks of the others were murkily visible behind an opaque veil. Like a curtain that dropped between the road and the woods. Keaton walked closer to it and held out a hand. To the others it was like watching a man place his palm against a window. He pushed, and nothing gave. There were small rivulets of moisture trickling down around him. He turned and looked at Jones.

"Damnedest thing," was all he said. Jones dropped the leather lead he'd been holding and met his friend. He touched the wall and drew back as though bitten. He drew a deeper breath and touched it again and this time allowed his hand to remain.

Behind his eyes a hundred images bombarded him: Screaming faces-men, women and children. Fires and smoke. Rivers of blood and seas of scabbing slop. Shining skin and insect legs. All of it wrapped in voices like black lung that wheezed and burned. Words so ancient they were before there was language. He opened his eyes and turned to Keaton.

"This is the edge of the door. One of them." He looked to the other side of the road and saw the same thing over there. "The bottom of it, I think."

"Then we need to keep going, find the keyhole and get it open." Keaton spoke with an uncertainty.

"I worry that it might already be open, and our job is to close and lock it."

Keaton's face went a shade paler. "Damn you."

"I also worry that our key might not be the key. That it might not be a key at all but just a strange bone we found. Maybe it is. Maybe not. I just feel unsure."

"But it sure looks like a key and it feels weird. Like all the rest of this nightmare we're in."

"That doesn't mean anything. I'm not sure anything does anymore."

"Damn you again." Keaton said with no trace of a smile. Jones stood and stared at the point where the road met the horizon. A cloak of smoky air that kissed the curve of the earth ahead of them. Atop the horse, Jubal cradled his sling. From within its folds came whispers that sounded like beetles under October leaves. *"The little one, brother."* The men heard it speak. Jubal gazed down into the creased cotton and nodded.

"If you're sure there ain't no other way," and then he looked at the men, a look of surprise on his face. A child caught getting into the sweets jar. "What?" he asked. No one said a thing as Jones bent to recover the lead and they began walking once again. Above them, something very large moved behind the clouds, like a face peeking through a sheer curtain. Somewhere in the distance something like thunder cracked, followed by a noise that sounded like deep laughter. They never slowed their pace.

JUBAL

48.

They'd made it as far as they could before the sun dropped away. Keaton dozed against a large rock that jutted from the edge of the road like a bone. Jones sat hunched by the feeble fire. Jubal had moved away from them, barely within the glow of the flames. He had his sling unfolded and laid across his lap. The larger sister sat on his thigh. The hair was a clotted mess that was thick as bramble. It hardly smelled anymore, that or they had all grown so rank it wasn't easy to notice. He leaned as far down as he could, his ear above the larger sister. Its side billowed and there were soft sounds coming from the small mouth. The eye on her opposite side rolled and rolled. Blue as ocean. Jubal listened and nodded. His eyes beginning to water. "Ain't no other way?" he whispered. More damp muttering from his lap. Jubal gently picked up the smaller sphere and gently lifted it to his lips and kissed it lightly. It was less hairy and lumpier than the larger one. It resembled a misshapen pear, the skin that covered it dented and gray. There was a small dimple of an eye that was open a crack but whatever lived beneath it was fish belly white and blind. It barely breathed. He rubbed it gingerly with his thumb and it trembled, emitting a low purring sound. "It's alright," the boy whispered, hardly audible. Jubal hooked his thumb into the spot where the eye was and pushed in with his thumbnail. The lid gave, and the digit slid under easily. Like it was an overripe orange or apple. He then bit his bottom lip and slid his thumb up and over the top of the small thing and the skin split and it peeled like rind. Viscous fluid trickled over his fingers as he pulled the skin down and under, removing it completely from the thing. He laid her down on his lap and wiped the slippery slime from his hands. The flesh beneath the indentation that would have become a mouth in a perfect world trembled, like a pouting child's face. He beheld the small skull on his thigh. It wasn't quite right but it was definitely a skull. But not of bone, more like a mushroom, pulpy and gray. He sniffed back tears as he then moved the larger sister over, almost against the smaller one and leaned in close. The small one still purred only it was very faint now and almost seemed to be a whimper. "I'm sorry, little sister. But this is the way, I'm told." And with that he nudged the smaller orb to the larger and as he did so the mouth of the larger one opened. Wider than it ever had. Wider than seemed possible. The teeth that filled it were fishhooks of white. She ate her sister in no more than two bites. Jubal sobbed quietly and once the chewing had stopped he could hear a soft thrum from within his sister. Like the ticking of a watch in a deep pocket. The little one was still purring. Jubal held his sister(s) to his ear and listened to the little one purr until he nodded off. Drying tears on reddened cheeks and a sad smile on his lips.

JONES, KEATON & JUBAL

49.

The night was a slug trail across the sky. Glistening and black. The fire had digested itself down to embers and floating sparks as the men and the boy slept around it. Jones had an arm up over his face as was his way. Keaton slept, seated and leaning against a log, that filthy hat pulled down over closed eyes. The rasp of his nasal breathing had grown louder than anything else. Off from them, the boy slept with the tumorous sphere of his sister in his hand, held close to his ear. They snored in unison. Enterline stood and chewed at the sour grass that grew here. She watched over them.

KEATON & JONES & JUBAL

50.

Keaton stood over by where the strange partition formed a barrier between them and the woods. He emptied his bladder, watching the sour yellow piss as it hit and ran down what looked to be thin air. He was alarmed that he didn't find it as alarming and strange as it most definitely was. These last days had proven to him that everything was tenuous, reality and the rules and regulations that guided and held sway over it. Months ago, he was a lousy man who wandered around and did odd jobs and slept in barns. Now he and a practical stranger and a kid with a sister that was a mouth in a ball of fucking hair were about to have a showdown with God-knows-what to stop more monsters from crashing through the sky into the world. He had inadvertently pinched off his flow and let go and finished his piss. He shook off and put himself away before he turned to head back to where the others were waking. He took a glance down the road from where they had come and stopped still. The road, or where there had been road, that they had walked in on, that was gone. The dirt and stone path was replaced by thick vines and choking branches. Talon-like thorns that ached for a taste of them. There were large black flowers here and there and they oozed like weeping sores. They smelled of gone-off meat and death. Keaton took a furtive side step towards the others and then sped it up until he was almost at a jog. Jones was up and standing, he looked up fast when he heard Keaton's gallop and turned to see where he was running from. He saw that the path had been eradicated by growth and his jaw dropped open a little. Jubal yawned and sat up, hastily slipping his sister back into her sling and adjusting it as he stood. "What the hell is that?" he yowled and pointed to the vile looking jungle that was a road only hours before. He took off his hat and scratched at the greasy hair that crowned his head.

"Think this has been happening behind us the whole time?"

"I'm not certain." Jones said, his voice wavered a bit.

"I think that I am. We're being herded. This is like a damn cattle chute. Like that damn spider I was telling you about. We can't go back and can't skirt off to the sides…nowhere but ahead." As Keaton's agitated banter flowed, flecks of white spittle dotted the filthy handkerchief tied around his throat.

"We was headed that way anyhow." Jubal spoke.

"True. But now it seems like it weren't our design. We got no controls now, Son. We can't do anything but what it expected of us. We just had the luck to not be in his path in any of these places. We're being drawn into something unknown and unprepared for. For a bit I felt all mighty, like we'd been picked for a special job…now it ain't quite like that. It ain't even like we planned any of it."

"Has it ever been another way?" Jones intoned as he adjusted his hat and untied Enterline from the log she was tethered to.

Keaton smirked. "One of these days, I'd love to smack the fuckin' riddles right outta you."

Jones smiled back. "I think I would too." He snicked through his teeth and the horse started to walk alongside him and Jubal as they stepped toward the remaining road, where Keaton was standing.

"I was just remembering a time when I went fishing with my father. So very long ago. I recall he caught a fish and I asked how it was that a fish could not see the hook tied to the twine. My Father said —'All it can see is an end to its hunger'— then he unhooked the fish and put on another worm and dropped it in the brook. He pulled another fish out almost right away. He looked at me and smiled and said —"We all have lines that bait us and most times we can eat the bait and remain free but you must know that for each of us there is a hook that is destined to meet our lip and we will most likely clearly see it and allow it to happen anyway." Jones nodded ahead, and they started walking.

"I'm just gonna smack them right outta you." Keaton grumbled and added: "Let's move on," as he unfastened his gun, just in case.

Behind them, the road was being devoured as they walked. Beside them, behind the clear walls, shadows cavorted, and long faces leered, tentacular tongues dangled. They kept their eyes forward and feet moving. The damned day stretched like drying hide.

LEVI

51.

He stood and watched the road into town. The corpse of the town. Wounds that bled smoke and debris into the artery of main street. Levi held his hands out before him and they shook like a divining rod. He looked up at the sky and there was a large section that looked different than the rest. Almost like a torn curtain allowing a peek through clear glass behind. The things that moved there, much more visible than ever before, were the stuff of nightmares and madness. The skin between worlds was so thin now it was almost like clear lake water. Through it were visible: enormous flanks of scale and chitin. Fingers as large as graveyard trees. Membranous wings and wide staring eyes. Eyes that leered and rolled over to a white so blinding it rivaled the moon at its fullest. So many of them. All pressed to that one sheer spot in the sky above. Only yards above the ground, like a trapdoor.

Levi beheld them and felt the pulse of the earth, the other things below. All of them impatient and almost frenzied. Squirming and somersaulting in the heart of the ground. "When?" he managed to articulate. The word being frail as alabaster that fell apart at its own harsh sound. He gagged and vomited up a reply in many voices at once:

"Soon. For they are nearly arrived."

"In a wink. In a wrinkle. In the time it takes a world to die."

"They come. They come."

"The tail goes in mouth—goes in mouth—goes in mouth."

"The Hottest of damnations is His smile."

Levi closed his aching eyes and tears ran down raw and veiny cheeks. Somewhere, deep in the maelstrom that was his soul, a tiny memory presented itself. Only a sliver. Something of three wise men with gifts on their way to greet a king.

JONES & KEATON & JUBAL

52.

He had been riding for nearly a day and a half and the fickle breeze had done little to scour the smell of smoke from his clothes and hair. In a way, he was glad as every whiff of that acrid sour smoke reminded him of Ford. That man had somehow managed to fill a void he'd had since he was a boy, in short time the man had built year's worth of reverence and adoration inside Jones where before was only crumbling bricks of pity and self-loathing. Jones licked his lips and tasted salt and smoke. He smiled and looked to the horizon. The sun slithered across it like a great worm. Jones wondered where he was going and what he was doing, really. It was easy to say he was out for revenge but was that true? He felt drawn, a bandage being pulled slowly from a wound, marred by pain and suffering but now free to flutter in the air. Except he didn't feel all that free either. Something was brewing. He felt, everything felt, like the calm before a storm. The air seemed pregnant with promises dark and horrible. The wind was a minimal trickle where once it tore through the valleys like stallions. The nights seemed to stretch longer, and the days just limped and whimpered. The slug in his chest thrummed like a bell, he felt it in his bones. It made his teeth itch. He closed his eyes and allowed it to guide him. He knew he needed to keep going and find Keaton. He hoped that would be soon. Enterline sped up in her trot, which could only mean food was ahead. His stomach hoped for the same.

"You hungry?"

Jones was pulled from his recollective daydreaming and looked up at the boy on his horse. "Pardon?"

"Your belly is growling something fierce." Jubal stated, his hand cupping the bulge of the sling against his side. Jones noticed there was a spot where there appeared to be blood seeping through the dirty cloth.

"I am a little. It can wait." He snuck a look over to Keaton who was staring at the sling as well. Keaton nodded, and Jones gave the leather lead a quick yank and Enterline stopped.

"Git down." he said to the boy, more sharply than he had intended. Jubal slid down from the back of the horse and stood looking at the two men.

"What's wrong?" Jubal asked.

"Git that thing off." Keaton spoke, his eyes squinted nearly closed as he chewed his lip.

"Go on, son." Jones urged, a little kinder than his previous command. "Then take off your shirt as well."

Jubal raised the sling over his head and held it out to Jones, as he stood closest. The man held it like it was a rotting sack of maggoty meat, the grimace on his face told all. The lump in the sling moved a little, and a hissing gasp emitted from the folds. Jubal didn't bother trying to unbutton the shirt, just yanked it up and over his head.

"Lord Almighty." Keaton sneered as he took quick steps to get to the boy. He gently touched the swelling wounds that lined his side. All along his ribs and up into the area beneath the armpit were round marks that looked like dark bruises. They were rimmed with small punctures that had crusted to scabs. The center of each wound held a raised bubble of bright yellow pus. Keaton delicately touched one of them blisters with a trembling finger and jerked back quickly. It was hot to the touch. Jubal didn't bat an eye. "Kid?" was all the man managed.

"I gotta feed her. She's my kin." He looked proud and ashamed at the same time. Jones looked up at the man and the boy. At the sores on the child's flesh and back to the sling. "Where's the other one?"

"What?" it was Keaton.

"The small one is missing."

"She ain't. She's still here." Jubal offered, pulling the shirt back down.

"Weren't there two of them things? Keaton asked.

"There was. Still is kinda. She is inside of Aggie now," he paused and almost smiled. "I named her after my Ma. Aggie told me that it was to be done. She ate her little sister so they could be stronger when we needed it." He looked at the men. The way they just stood gawping like wide-eyed fish yanked from their brook. "I peeled her like an orange and Aggie ate her all up. They got ideas or a plan to follow, it seems." He reached out for the sling and Jones made no move at all so the boy just lifted it from his arm and put it back on.

Keaton's voice was a rusted thing: "Ideas?"

"I don't know. She just tells me things. Has for a while now. Mostly when we're sleeping. She sounds like ma, soft and warm in my ear. I love hearing her." His smile stumbles a little, nearly falls flat out but rights itself. "We're going the right way. We're supposed to go. We have an appointment. We're to nail the door closed and break the lock."

"Let me set things to a point here, if I may." Keaton strode up to where Jones and the horse were standing, pushing his dank hat up further on his head. "We were rambling not going much of anywhere. Jones was doing the same but kinda looking for me as he wanted to put me six feet down. There's a man what's killing towns and them dead towns are forming the edges of some damned door that's going to open and let all these giant monsters in? It's up to us to close it?!" Keaton laughed, and it was a crazed thing. "I got it right? That's the gist?!"

"Sounds about right," the boy nodded, his calm acceptance was unsettling.

The men looked at one another and then at the boy. Jubal offered another smile, a weak one at that. "How's it going to go down?"—This time it was Jones.

"The only way it can, that is what Aggie said to tell you. She said you was gonna ask me that." Jubal rubbed the lump in the sling and a soft mewl rose from within. Jones just swallowed and shook his head. Above them the sun was muted by thick smoke and fog. The air didn't move at all. Keaton kicked at the dirt.

"Let's get on with it then, not polite to keep destiny waiting," Jones urged.

KELLIANNE

53.

She watched the man standing in the middle of what used to be a street. A place where coach and team moved through. Where people meandered. Now it was just desolate space that was fenced by smoldering ruins and crumpled bodies. She stood on the hill, under the trees and looked down into the small valley, over and onto the corpse of Lansdale and watched the man. He held up too long arms and howled like a beast at the sky. She saw shadows swim behind the clouds. Felt things move beneath the earth, reverberating through the pads of her paws. She put her nose to the ground and smelled the sour reek of blood and earth. Her tongue darted out of her mouth to taste the gaggingly thick air and she did just that. She kept her head low and went back to watching the thing that was once a man. He was removing his coat and hat. He had horns that were fingers. He had scales on his arms. His chest was ringed with nipples and scars. He was a monster. The very type the word had been invented for. She slowly and quietly laid in the dusty underbrush and kept watching for them. Waiting. She wasn't sure for what exactly, she just knew that she was to be here and she would know what to do when the time came. She closed her eyes and remembered Bob, and if a wolf could smile, she did that, sadly, as she dozed, uneasily.

JUBAL, KEATON & JONES

54.

The woods started to atrophy and wither until they gave way and opened into pastures of drying grass, dank yellow like the color of elderly eyes. Jones made a shushing noise and the horse slowed. The boy on her back sat up and rubbed his eyes.

"We there?" he asked. No one answered him. The road had widened a bit and Keaton bent and picked up a stone which he then threw off to the side of the road. It made a sound like a penny in a wishing well as it pinged off the invisible wall. Keaton shook his head and commenced his walking. Jones looked ahead and through a veil of smoke was able to make out ragged edges that may have been buildings a while ago. He swallowed hard and felt a burn in his belly.

"I believe we might be." They stopped and stared for minutes that moved at a snail's pace. The only sound was the crackling of dying flames and the groaning of scorched timber. It sounded like the wheeze of the dying. Another less-than-good omen.

LEVI

55.

The sigh that escaped the ruins of his lips was rapturous. He could hardly see through the wash of tears that slicked his lidless eyes. What had happened to his eyelids anyway? He frowned, and the scabs tore loose, fresh blood flowing over his chin. "They're here," he said, possibly out loud. He stood and opened his arms in a welcoming manner, his gun held firmly in his right hand, finger curled around the trigger, the flesh so swollen and raw sausage pink that it filled the guard. Levi watched as the men and the boy on the horse slowly grew as they approached. He managed to get one lone thought out before the maelstrom of voices rose and drowned it all out. *I shall be released*, was that thought. He was shaking, and tears continued to flee from his stinging eyes. With a skinless thumb he cocked the hammer and shook his head. He might have been laughing. It was all so nebulous anymore.

KEATON & JONES & JUBAL

56.

"Jubal, you'll stay here with Enterline while Jones and I go on out there and face that bastard." Keaton was trying hard to sell his valor, but it was of little use. The fact he was soaked with sweat and his voice quaked like a leaf in a storm betrayed his true demeanor. He was terrified.

"I want to—" Jones stepped forward and shook his head.

"You will stay here and guard my horse." He punctuated the statement with a look of severity that the kid didn't question. He simply nodded and stood with his hand on the horse's neck. Enterline nibbled at some weeds growing by the ruins of the stables. They were oily and yellow and could not have tasted good. Keaton looked to Jones and they nodded and started out into the fog that was really a wall of rolling smoke. Keaton paused and looked back to where the shadows of the boy and horse were—

"If we don't come back. You take that horse and go back the way we came, if you can. If not, go forward. Find yourself a good place where you can start over." Keaton tried to smile but his lips couldn't clear his teeth. There was no spit to lubricate anything in that mouth of his. No one said anything else and the men went off to fight a monster, while a boy and a horse hid in shadows and smoke in a dead town under a broken sky.

KEATON & JONES & LEVI

57.

The two men scurried more than strutted down the center of the street. Frantic mice in the farmer's kitchen. The smoke flowed over them in thick stinking waves that made their eyes water. As they reached what would have been the square of the town a week ago, they stopped.

"I've been waiting," a voice boomed from the fog. It was wet and thick. After tearing off the strands of lip that dangled and snagged his teeth and tongue, he found he could speak in a decipherable manner. If he took his time and spoke slow. Neither man responded.

"A little too late to play coy, I think." This was followed by laughter. Rich and deep and very moist.

"We don't know you. Know nothing of you." Keaton tried to reply.

"You do and you don't."

"What's that mean?"

"Just what it means. You have no idea who I am but you sure as hell know of me."

"We aren't even sure what this is about?" Jones asked.

"A birth." Levi sucked in a breath and they heard it: a broken bellows. "I made a womb with my own bare hands. Gigantic and bloody and through it the masters will come. Them behind the voices. God, to finally get them out of my head and my heart." He looked up to the sky and the men followed his gaze. The sky was darkening, ripe plum like a threat of storm. All but a piece directly above them, that remained uncluttered by cloud or smoke and was a clear pond in black earth. It was like a tear-shaped window, and through it horrors were visible. Dark green and blackened. Oily and scaled. Eyes. Teeth and things that swirled and squirmed. Jones looked back to the large man before them and then to Keaton.

"I'm not sure what hell you're trying to call down. We want nothing to do with it. And I aim to kill you if that'll stop it."

"Shit, we'll kill you even if it won't," Keaton added. His own gun drawn and aimed at the bulky silhouette before them.

Keaton cocked the gun and just as he started to apply pressure to the trigger he was hit in the face with something. It was sharp and slimy and knocked him to the ground. His gun fell as he flung his hands up to guard his head.

"It might be that easy," that septic voice spoke over him. Levi was on him. Heavy as stone and sharp. He had extra joints and his limbs were tipped in point.

"Keaton!!" Jones shouted but the smoke had disoriented him, and he sounded far off. Keaton opened his eyes and saw that face up close and right over his. That mouth was a groundhog burrow lined with teeth over every size and shape. The throat twisted and went on forever. He saw the ruins of a nose, now like a smaller mouth above the other that just oozed mucous and bloody froth. He stopped looking when he got to the eyes. Widely-set and different colors. One was white and pink and dead; the other was river muck black. That one had no white. Just black with a blue center. Keaton gasped, and the distraction afforded Levi the time to get a deep lunge into the man's side. He felt his ridged knuckles grate on rib and heard the man groan.

"Your pa said to tell you howdy." Levi sneered and touched Keaton's nose with the tip of his wormy tongue. Keaton went blind with rage and the pain of the blow and raised his own hand and drove his left thumb deep into that pink eye.

"Don't you say it!" he seethed. "Don't you dare mention my pa!"

He pushed as hard as he could and felt the nail violate the eyeball, the fluid squirting onto his stubbled cheeks and dribbling down over his knuckles. He pushed deeper until the tip of his thumb met brain and then even more. He kept pushing until Levi managed to land another punch to his side, the sound of breaking ribs coupled with the white-hot spear of agony and his breath was a rabbit in a snare. Frantic but stalled.

"Don't you fucking dare." Keaton drooled as his vision swam away and he sank deep into the quicksand of unconsciousness.

KEATON

58.

He felt his life leaking away. Or at least he felt that he should be feeling that, but he didn't. There was pain, but he'd been swaddled in that particular feeling for so long that it hardly registered anymore. He touched his side where Levi had hit him, so very hard, and felt bone and hot blood. His ribs had come through the flesh like dog's teeth. He groaned and rolled to his other side and made to stand up. He felt something poking his other side and slid a hand into the pocket of his vest. He removed the bone key and gripped it in a shaking fist. He looked back over his shoulder and saw the large shadow of Levi standing there. Keaton rolled quicker and launched himself as upright as he could. He grabbed for his gun and realized too late it was gone, somewhere on the ground, somewhere in the haze of smoke. He spit, and it was tangy blood. He drew a deep and painful breath and stood tall as he could. He stepped forward and swung hard at the side of Levi's head. He heard his knuckles shatter on impact, like rock candy. But the key connected with the big man's temple where it jutted like a branch beside the waggling finger that sprouted there.

Levi smiled, and it was an impossible smile. The corners, what were actually ragged tears in his cheeks, went all the way to his ears. The smile itself just an unorganized chorus of bones and teeth, different sizes and shades of brown, black and white. It reminded Keaton of Indian corn. He held his throbbing hand and mewled as he hobbled backwards from the lumbering thing that just kept smiling and stepped his way. Levi broke off the key and dropped the end to the ground. The finger horn began to push the broken end further into the wound. Keaton snuck a glance over his shoulder and saw Jones a few yards away, gun drawn and steadily aimed in their direction.

"Shoot!" he howled before he fell and counted two seconds before the shot rang out.

KEATON & JONES

59.

Keaton lay over by a pile of charred crates, the fruit scattered around them bleeding juices. The ragged hole in his side was a gasping mouth, drawing wet breaths.

"I broke the key. Right off in his head." He tried to yell. Jones nodded but kept walking towards Levi in a steady gait. Levi stood as straight as he could, still stooped under the weight of all the added flesh and warping of his body. Levi opened his mouth to scream and voices flooded out in a cacophonous hymn. The sky above them grew darker, the spot that was like a window bulged like a blister. Tiny globules of ichor seemed to be dribbling and raining down upon them. It was tearing. A womb about to spew. Levi drew back a monstrous arm, a fist tipped in bone ready to kiss Jones on the mouth. Jones fired his gun. Then he fired again. Levi let the punch go free.

KEATON & JUBAL

60.

The sky was rended and things were starting to come through. Stepping into the world on legs long and spindly, flying through with waspy wings and mandibles dripping. Eyes as large as wagon wheels. Jubal ducked low and reached into the sling, he patted Aggie and slid his thumb into her moist mouth; she suckled it like a teat. Jubal cowered behind the desiccated remains of a stagecoach that had fallen near the gutter. There was a woman face down in the water trough; her red hair floated like lily pads. He squinted hard to see, having trouble what with the tears that drowned his eyes. He slowly sidled over to the figure on the ground.

Reaching toward the man who had taken him into his care, tried to look out for him and help him. The man who was now spilling his life into the dirt of a town where Hell had literally erupted. Jubal squirmed over closer and laid a small hand on Keaton's shoulder.

"Keaton?"

"Yeah, son." His voice was wet crepe paper.

"I don't know what to do." The words came out in a sobbing jumble. His chest hitching as they did so.

Keaton forced a smile, the blood rimming his lips making him look like a circus clown.

"No one does. I broke the key." He paused and tried to capture a breath. "Don't think it'll matter much. Ain't much to do. I'm pretty well gone, son. You just stay hid." He tried to breathe again. It was a wriggling snake in wet hands. Air escaping from the holes in his lungs faster than he could suck it in.

"You just stick with Jones. And be smart. You grow to be that man you know you should be, not the one anyone tells you to be." He smiled, but it was weak, a crooked painting on a cracked wall. They sat quiet for a spell, as quiet as it can be on the lip of Hell with a man fighting a monster while demons tear into the world just yards away.

"Thank you, Keaton." Jubal whispered and squeezed the man's shoulder. The man reached up and took the hand in his own thick fingered one and squeezed. Once.

"No. I believe I oughta thank you." He closed his eyes and the smile stayed in place as the last breath wheezed its way from the wound in his side, rising in the smoky dusk like a battlefield wraith. Jubal hung his head and bawled just as quietly as he could. Holding Keaton's hand until it was frigid.

JONES & LEVI

61.

Levi swung and Jones ducked but came back up swinging hard into Levi's jaw. The skin tore away like rotten sponge and with it went most of the flesh beneath. Levi roared but it was stitched with laughter. The big man shook Jones from him like a dog shrugging off an attacking tick. Levi rose to his full height and scanned the ground for his gun. It lay in the dust a dozen or so feet away. Jones stood beside it and following Levi's line of vision, secured it to the earth under one boot. He had his own gun drawn and pointed at Levi. The giant smiled and spat something black and wriggling onto the ground. Above them things were squeezing through the hole in the sky. Stepping over the two of them like they were ants in a sugar bowl— a nuisance to be dealt with at a later time. Levi looked up at them and smiled and closed his eyes. He dropped his arms to his side and took a few quick steps in the direction of Jones. Jones fired. A hole opened in the larger man's neck. It sprayed blood, but Levi kept walking. His smile growing. Jones fired again and again. Levi gained an extra eye in the center of his forehead and bid farewell to most of his nose. He smiled and kept coming.

With the fourth shot, Levi stumbled and fell to his knees. The wound above his sternum drooled thick black blood. Levi laughed, and it was a sincere sound. He looked at Jones and his eyes, though hidden under the wash of gore from the hole in his head, were shining. Levi sat back on his haunches and dragged a large hand up over his face, clearing a swath in the red that coated it. Jones stood still and cocked his gun again.

Levi nodded and tried to stand but couldn't do it. Instead, he leaned forward, and frog jumped in the other man's direction. Jones pulled the trigger. The shot hitting him in the same place as earlier, the hole in his throat spreading wider and causing Levi's head to tilt sideways hanging oddly from the sides where the remaining flesh still anchored it. Levi started to rise. An obelisk of blood and suffering. He had made it to his knees when the small shadow ran between the two. The boy with an arm outstretched. The boy who screamed at the top of his lungs. Levi opened his mouth to laugh and nearly raised an arm before the child slammed into him, shoving something small and round into the wound that was his neck. Once nestled in, Aggie started to chew. Her small mouth was a whir of tiny teeth and screeching. Bloody froth foamed up around her as she dug deeper and deeper in. Levi's eyes popped, and he worked his mouth like a gasping trout. Levi grabbed at his throat as he fell over, an overwhelming amount of blood soaking his neck and chest. Jones took a step closer and pointed the gun at the man on the ground.

"We had the key." Jones huffed as he tried to fill his lungs.

"That weren't no key." Levi chuckled with almost no sound. Thick red spray pouring from his mouth as Aggie worked her way down his esophagus, neck bulging like a snake swallowing a rat. He coughed once and waved a hand, feebly.

"We was the key. This, right here was the key." He sighed and pointed to the thing that was burrowing deeper into him. The noise that floated from his mouth sounded rapturous.

"I'm almost free," he hissed and fell still. Jones stood and kept the gun on him for a good while as he listened to the voices that flowed from his drying lips like rats fleeing a burning barn. The clicking of those awful little teeth as they sheared through the monster's innards. He looked up at the sky. The window was gone, the sky a solid gray wall now. He scanned the horizon and saw no evidence of the horrors that had come through into their world. His brow furrowed as he slowly slid the gun in its holster. Levi was finally silent and through the hole in his chest, a small blood-slicked ball emerged. Sides undulating. Jubal picked her up and held her to his cheek, the red coming off like a whore's lipstick. He held his sister and looked to Jones. Jones held out a hand and the pair turned and made their way to where Keaton lay.

JUBAL & JONES

62.

"He was a good man." Jones spoke as he knelt and wiped the blood from his dead friend's lips.

"He was. I sometimes wished he were my Pa."

"I think he might have done the same."

"I'm glad you didn't kill him." Jubal said.

"Me too. "

They stood in the belly of the corpse of Lansdale. Covered in blood and soot and drowning in oceans of regret.

The pair stood and watched the spot where the enormous things that had stepped through the sky. Elephantine beasts that were somewhere climbing mountains and drinking rivers or punching deep holes into the bosom of the earth. Or perhaps they never were. Reality was an alien thing. Jones stood and stared at him silently for a long time before bending and hoisting him over his shoulder and carrying him to the end of the street where they had tethered Enterline. Jubal walked a few paces behind, whispering into the folds of the sling and crying as he did so.

"I'll miss him too," he said softly.

JUBAL & JONES

63.

The hole was not as deep as he deserved, but Jones was weary and just couldn't give much more. And Jubal, though he made valiant effort, wasn't much help. Jones lowered Keaton into the grave and looked to the boy and nodded. Jubal removed the sling from his neck and laid it on the ground. He cradled Aggie in his palm like some vile fruit. Bringing her to his lips he kissed the furred thing and held it to his ear. He nodded through a fresh crop of tears that ran from his eyes and leaned forward to drop Aggie into the crater of Keaton's chest. They both stared and while he couldn't be sure, Jones thought he saw the thing burrow deeper into the dead man before he started flinging armfuls of dirt on top of them.

"Aggie said she'd keep him company." Jubal offered as Jones worked.

Jubal turned, his back to the grave, sang as Jones finished filling in the grave, covering the boy's sister and their friend. A song his mother used to sing when he was a baby.

"*Onward, upward doth He beckon; Onward, upward would we press...*"

The sun faded and became the moon. It was full on night by the time Jones was done and the grave full. The tired man took the boy's hand, and with the horse, they headed out. Before long they were joined by another, a wolf with very sad eyes.

"Hello, Kellianne," Jones spoke, and the wolf pushed her head into his hand. He stroked her muzzle and smiled.

"Jones, is it done?" Jubal asked.

"I'm not sure. I don't even rightly know what happened. I know we lost a good man, we set another free from his demons. And we closed the window."

"But I saw monsters coming through."

"I did too, I thought, but I'm not sure where they got to. Maybe we dreamed them?"

"Like they was in our heads or our hearts."

"That's usually where the scariest monsters live."

"Maybe it didn't happen, and we dreamed it," Jubal tacked on.

Kellianne walked over the side where Jubal walked and licked his hand. He laughed and patted her head. Jones looked down into her eyes and opened his mouth to speak.

"No, it did but what and all I have no idea. I know we lost a friend. Two for me. But if you plan to stick with us that's a gain." The wolf looked at him and then the boy. A small whimpering bark was all she gave. He lightly gripped the fur of her neck. She stopped and looked up into his very tired face.

"I'll take a 'for now' then." He smiled and patted her and they started off again. Together, they walked the darkness down.

KEATON'S GRAVE

64.

The air was still and the sunshine warm. The winter had come in and rolled out and the spring was stretching its arms. The grave had sunken a little, but the grass was growing in. Kisses of green amidst a snow-scorched terrain. Near the center of the mound, something strange was blooming. Small and thin, five little fingers on a little hand. As the sunlight swallows the area, the fingers wiggle slightly, like petals grasping at the nourishing warmth of the sun..

ABOUT THE AUTHOR

John Boden lives a stones throw from Three Mile Island with his wonderful wife and sons. A baker by day, he spends his off time writing or watching old television shows. He likes Diet Pepsi and sports ferocious sideburns. He loves heavy metal and old country music, shoofly pie and old westerns.

He's a pretty nice fella, honest.

His work has appeared in *Borderlands 6*, *Shock Totem*, *Splatterpunk*, *Lamplight*, *Blight Digest*, the John Skipp edited *Psychos* and others. His not-really-for-children children's book, Dominoes has been called a pretty cool thing. His other books, *Jedi Summer With the Magnetic Kid* and *Detritus In Love* are out and about. He recently released a novella with fellow author Chad Lutzke called *Out Behind the Barn*.

He has a slew of things on the horizon

Curious about other Crossroad Press books?
Stop by our site:
http://www.crossroadpress.com
We offer quality writing
in digital, audio, and print formats.

Made in the USA
Monee, IL
13 August 2023

40948136R00095